SECRET VOW

WILLOW FOX

SECRET VOW

Mafia Marriages Book One

Willow Fox

Published by Slow Burn Publishing

eBook cover by Slow Burn Publishing

Paperback cover by MiblArt

© 2021

v2

1

DANTE

The way she dances does things to me that I know are wrong.

I swallow back another glass of whiskey, trying to suppress the urge to stalk over and capture her lips with mine.

"Tell me you're not considering sleeping with Nicole DeLuca," Moreno says.

He's my second, my best friend, and also blatantly honest, even when I don't want him to be.

He also knows that I've sported a hard-on for Nicole since the moment I learned of Gino's daughter.

I like a challenge, and she's off-limits. It makes the catch that much more fun.

"Have you seen me so much as talk to her?" I shoot Moreno a glare to shut the hell up. Somehow, I doubt he will do as I want.

He's a good guy if such a thing can be said about the Ricci Family.

"You keep drinking and staring. She's bound to notice you," Moreno says.

Maybe that's the point. I want her to notice me. I want her to fear me like her father, Gino, fears my family.

Nicole struts onto the dance floor. The light cascades across her raven hair.

She bumps and grinds, arms tossed into the air.

I want to fuck that smile right off her gleeful face.

She's a force to be reckoned with, and I'm just the man to turn her life upside down.

"Have another drink. It's on me." Moreno gestures to the bartender, and he waltzes over and pours another whiskey.

"On you?" I laugh.

I own the damned bar.

He can offer to buy me all the drinks he wants. I drink here for free.

"Doesn't mean you shouldn't tip the staff." Moreno slides a fifty to the bartender, Ren-something.

I forget her name. I hired her after the last guy caused me a headache and a dead boss.

Some things are better left in the past.

Being don has its advantages, including getting any girl I want.

Tonight, that girl is Nicole DeLuca.

I shift on the barstool.

Usually, I claim the corner booth. It has a reserved placard for the occasion that I might want to come in and have a drink or business with an associate.

"You need another girl. Someone less deadly," Moreno says.

I laugh under my breath and sip my whiskey. "You talk like she's an assassin."

"Her father is."

I wave my hand in the air. "He's an old man, Gino. Pain in my ass." He is also a problem that needs taking care of, but that's a job for another day.

Tonight, I'm here to cut off some steam and have fun.

"You fuck that girl, and he'll hunt you down," Moreno warns. He gestures the bartender over and gets himself a drink.

I raise an eyebrow. I haven't seen Moreno drink in, well, since forever.

This is bad if he's drinking. "Shit, I'm driving you to drink. It really must be the end of the world," I mock.

He pinches the bridge of his crooked nose. He got that from defending my honor in a bar fight nearly two decades ago. I'd been young, naïve, and on the cusp of seventeen. I knew how to fight like a kid, not like a man.

Moreno rectified that. He taught me everything I know about the family business.

"Just promise me that you'll leave her alone." Moreno sips his whiskey.

It's obvious to anyone who knows him he can't stand the taste, but he drinks like a pro to an outsider.

"You don't have to kill yourself for me," I joke and point at the whiskey. "I'll down that if you're struggling."

"Do you see me struggling?" Moreno asks.

"While you enjoy that whiskey, I'm going to work my moves on the dance floor."

"Dante," Moreno says my name, but his tone holds more than just a hint of warning.

He's screaming at me to listen to him.

But when do I ever listen?

The funny thing is that I'm his boss, and I don't take orders from Moreno or anyone else. While I appreciate his concern, that's all it is to me, and I'm going to do whatever the hell I want.

Hasn't he realized that yet?

I climb off the barstool and make my way onto the dance floor. I don't dance. There's no need.

I'm on a mission, and she is my target.

We lock eyes, and she blushes on my approach.

Good. She doesn't seem to know me. At least she hasn't indicated that I'm the bastard trying to kill her father.

"I'm here with friends," she says like that line will work to shoo me away.

"Nice of them to ditch you," I say.

She's been dancing for the last forty or so minutes, alone. The handful of guys who tried to pick her up haven't had any luck.

One of them looks at me apologetically.

I've yet to see her with a shot or drink in her hand, either.

"How do you know they're not in the bathroom?" Nicole asks.

"If they are, they must have snuck out the window."

She rolls her eyes. "Are you implying that I'm that boring?"

"On the contrary, I'm implying nothing, only that you're a pretty woman dancing alone."

"I'll bet that line works on all the other girls," Nicole says.

She's right. It doesn't take much for them to fall at my feet. I'm blessed with good looks and a great body. Does she not notice?

"How about I buy you a drink, and if you never want to see me again—"

"Okay."

Her response takes me by surprise.

I lead her toward the reserved booth and gesture for her to climb in first. The booth is curved, and I make sure to sit close beside her, our thighs touching.

I want to touch her, seduce her, and bring her all sorts of heightened pleasure.

"Are you sure we should be sitting here?" Nicole asks. "It did say reserved."

I merely shrug. I don't want to give away who I am, especially if she's unaware of my position of power. She shouldn't know.

"Let's see what happens," I say.

She raises a curious eyebrow but shuts her mouth.

The bartender from earlier comes over, and I gesture for two drinks—one for each of us. I don't have to give the bartender my order. She gets the finest liquor, top-shelf from the collection.

"I never got your name," Nicole says.

"Daniel," I answer. It's a lie. I've always been Dante.

It's clear she doesn't recognize me, and I can't have my name triggering any further recognition.

"I'm Nikki," she says and rests a hand on my thigh.

Her tune has changed since I met her minutes ago on the dance floor, but I'm not sure why. Do I care?

"It's lovely to meet you, Nikki," I say, as if I'm trying to remember her name.

I could never forget it. I've had my eye on her since she strolled into town and moved in with her daddy, my number one enemy: Gino DeLuca.

All I've wanted is to take him down, and in the process, I'll be forced to ruin her for other men.

Too bad.

She's beautiful, with her long black hair and deep-set amber eyes.

Cute and sexy.

And she could have a normal life if I wasn't at war with her old man.

The lights are dim, the bar not terribly crowded for a Friday night.

The music slows, and I'm glad we're already in the booth. While a slow dance is nice at times, it doesn't fit right now. Not when I want to grind against her.

The bartender returns with two drinks. One is a whiskey for me and the second a whiskey sour on the rocks for her. It's strong but sweet, too girly for my taste, but the ladies haven't turned it away in the past.

I don't expect her to be any different.

But I'm wrong.

She slides her glass toward me and grabs mine before I can lift it to my lips. "I'll have what you're having."

She means my glass of whiskey.

Damn, that shit is expensive.

The girls always get the off-label, and since it's mixed, they can't taste the difference.

She smiles coyly and bats her long, dark lashes, but it's just an act.

What game is she playing tonight?

"Hope you don't mind. I prefer the good stuff, liquid gold." Nicole gulps the whiskey in a matter of seconds and slams the glass down hard on the wooden table.

Her warm amber gaze has flecks of gold, and the longer she watches me, the more I fall into her stare.

What the hell is going on?

"Do you want to get out of here?"

I do more than anything, but my gut is telling me no. "How about I take you back to your place?" I suggest.

I already know she's living with her father, but I wonder what excuse she'll give me.

2

FOUR HOURS EARLIER

NICOLE

"Come down here for a moment, Nicole," Papa says.

I'm his pet, his prize he likes to tout around to suitors in the business. He brags about how proud he is of me, but he's only proud of himself.

I hate my father but he's family. Moving home wasn't my idea, but I don't have anywhere else to go without a job and after recently graduating from college.

I stroll down the staircase. My bare feet graze over the cold wood floor. "Yes, Papa?"

"Come, sit with me in my office."

Dread flows straight to my stomach. Anytime my papa wants me to join him in his office, it means I've disappointed him in some way or another.

What have I done this time?

"As you know, I've held my tongue and let you chase a degree and graduate from that foolish school of yours," Papa says.

My cheeks burn, and I press my lips tight together to keep from reacting emotionally.

"Now that you're home and you're twenty-two, you are going to settle down with a young man of my choosing."

"Papa!" I feel like a child interrupting him.

And he treats me as such.

His hand slaps me hard across the face.

"Do not interrupt me," he scolds.

I hang my head in shame. It's what he wants, after all, control.

"I've thought long and hard about the business, Nicole. It's in everyone's best interest if you are wed to—"

"No!" I won't hear it. I wait for him to slap me again across the face, but it doesn't come. "I'm not marrying someone who you think I ought to marry. That's such an archaic notion!" I shout in disgust as I hurry out of his office.

"Young lady, I'm not through speaking with you!"

I don't care, and he gets the message as I hurry for the front door. I slip on a pair of shoes and bolt out the main entrance.

I didn't think this through.

I have no car.

No money.

And no one to call or depend on.

I head for the main road, ignoring the guards as they question me on my way out, asking if I need a ride. As much as I want one, I also know that they will tell my papa everything, including where I've run off to.

————

I head for the bar in the nearest town. The walk doesn't bother me. The weather is nice, sunny and pleasant, which is better than my mood.

I want to get plastered, but I forgot my wallet. I could flirt with the bartender or maybe a hottie at the bar. That assumes anyone in this freakishly small town is handsome and worth my time.

It doesn't help that I have nowhere to go. Returning home weighs on me like a ton of bricks.

I skip the drinks and stroll out onto the dance floor. The pulse-pounding music wakes me up inside and makes me forget about the turbulent day. I shrug off the first two guys who vie for my attention.

They don't hold my interest. They're too smiley and picture-perfect.

There's a man at the bar who's hot.

Sharply dressed, dark eyes, and fit under his suit.

He's trying too hard to impress the ladies.

My gaze lingers on him longer than I intend to, and I break away, turning as I dance in the middle of the floor, my feet stomping on the ground. Cutting loose feels wonderful.

If only I could cut all ties to my life.

It wouldn't be so hard if I'd have landed a teaching job. My degree was a piece of paper, worthless.

I should have examined the job market before graduating with a degree in elementary education. It wasn't like I couldn't get a job. A few areas were hiring, but they weren't in the best neighborhoods.

That didn't overly concern me.

It was the fact rival families ran those territories.

I would always be a target so long as my father was don.

He hadn't always been don, but he'd been second in command, the underboss to Angelo DeLuca for years. I couldn't remember a time when Angelo and Papa weren't chummy.

When Angelo died, Papa took over the family business with pride and admiration.

He'd been a bastard to me when he'd been an underboss. I shudder at the memory of his hand slapping me across the face. Papa had never been gentle, but he also had left me well enough alone.

Now that he was Don DeLuca, the darkness that settled in his heart grew.

He wanted to be feared by everyone.

The handsome stranger with a dark and mysterious look to him strolls up to me. He doesn't pretend to dance. Surprisingly, he doesn't bump and grind against me, either.

I wouldn't have minded it if I had a few drinks in me first.

His name is Daniel. It rolls off my tongue with simplicity to it. He doesn't look like a Daniel, but what do I know?

He flirts and I finally take the bait. The truth is I need a ride out of this city, and if it means lifting his car keys or his wallet, so be it.

I join him for a drink, steal his whiskey, and the next thing I know, I'm asking if he wants to get out of here.

I can't go back home, even if I wanted to. A part of me wants to drag him in front of Papa and humiliate my father.

"They're fumigating my place," I lie so easily. I can't let him know I'm the daughter of Don DeLuca. I don't know who works for my papa and who he has crossed. He's made enemies. That's no secret. The DeLucas don't make friends easily.

"Funny, that's what's happening to my place," Daniel says.

I smile, shaking my head. "You are something else." I poke his chest. I'm not sure why or what comes over me, but I have the insistent need to feel something other than anger and resentment.

I hate my papa.

I grab Daniel by the tie and yank him toward me for a kiss.

I take him by surprise. Most men aren't used to my forcefulness and brashness. I'm used to power, others wielding it over me. It feels nice for a chance to be in control.

I swear I hear him growl.

Gosh, I want to devour him.

"I have a better idea," Daniel whispers against my ear and pulls me onto his lap.

I'm wearing a short black dress that cuts above the knee. I've got spaghetti straps that keep sliding down my shoulders, and for the first time tonight, I don't bother trying to pick them back up.

I can feel his heat poking me from beneath.

My fingers claw through his hair as our lips melt together.

He's not the only one growling. I think I just made a sound in unison.

We shouldn't.

We can't.

Not in the bar.

Not in a public place where anyone can see what we're doing.

God, I want him.

He bites down on my bottom lip and I moan.

The music covers my noises, but I'm sure Daniel can hear every sound that I make.

He guides my legs apart, and he explores what's hidden beneath my skirt. He feels over my panties. Can he tell they're soaked because of him?

His fingers are rough and quick, pushing my panties to the side. I'm not sure he didn't rip the silk material.

His lips move to my ear, his breath tickling and arousing me. "You're wet for me, Kitten."

The way he says it sends a shudder through my body.

He pinches my clit, sending a shockwave through me straight to my core.

I struggle to focus, to keep my eyes open. My breathing has deepened. Each breath comes out a gasp.

He covers my mouth, hot and rough, and he shifts my hips slightly, just enough to lift me off him while he guides his cock out from his trousers.

And then he's forceful, penetrating me.

I moan, confident the entire bar can hear the sounds, and everyone knows what we're doing.

Daniel covers my mouth. His tongue explores my lips as he grinds his hips and his hands rest on my hips.

We move together in unison. His thrusts are deep and strong.

Suddenly, he lifts my hips and turns me around to sit on his lap. He enters me again, my insides pulsating from the sensation of growing close and him momentarily pulling away.

I open my mouth to ask what he's doing, but he's already buried inside my warmth and wetness.

His movements turn faster, rougher as he pounds into me and I clench on.

"Not yet," he commands.

I gasp and feel on the edge of oblivion.

The sensation builds inside me. My heart is slamming against my ribcage, my breath coming out in pants as I'm coated in sweat.

I tremble and clench down on his member, and he grabs my chin and yanks my head to the side to face him.

"Did I tell you that you could come?" he asks. His tone is harsh.

I flinch at his words. I'm waiting for him to hit me, but he doesn't.

"I haven't yet." I'm tinkering on the edge.

"Fuck," he says.

Several more thrusts, and he's swelling inside me, on the brink.

"Come for me, Kitten."

I do as he commands, clenching down, squeezing him as I tremble on his lap. I bite down on my bottom lip, tugging it between my teeth to keep my moans at bay.

Daniel lifts me off his frame and sits me back down on the bench beside him. He adjusts himself back into his slacks and zips himself up. His eyes shine as he climbs out of the booth that we shared.

"Wait," I say and grab him by the tie. I pull him tight for one last kiss.

But that's not all I'm after. I need his keys or wallet. Whatever I can get my hands on first without him noticing.

With one hand latched to his tie, I'm careful to pickpocket him without him suspecting anything.

I shove his keys behind my back and am careful not to jingle them.

"Have a good night," I say with a coy smile.

He saunters across the room to the bar where his friend is situated. He sits down, and I slip out of the booth and skirt out the front door before Daniel can realize I stole his keys and call the cops.

3

DANTE

"Are you ready to get out of here?" I ask Moreno.

He looks bored, and I'm done now that I've had my fun.

My gaze scours over the bar, but I don't see any sign of Nicole. She must have already left. I'm not sure why I care. At least there aren't other men dancing with her.

A strange pang of jealousy hits me like lightning.

I shouldn't care. I gesture to the bartender for one more whiskey.

"I'm driving," Moreno says and holds out his hand.

He's waiting for me to deposit my keys into his palm.

"Fair enough." I'm in no mood to fight him and, quite frankly, a little more than tipsy. I don't need to get behind the wheel and crash my truck. Besides, that's why I have good men like Moreno accompany me.

Occasionally, I have chauffeurs too. But I like driving, getting behind the wheel and being in complete control. There's something that can be said for going off road, through rocky terrain, and across dangerous valleys all alone.

I swallow down the last glass of whiskey the bartender brings me.

She's cute.

Young. Barely twenty-one.

Hell, Nicole barely looked old enough to be in the bar.

Since when did I start chasing ass who was nearly half my age?

Fuck.

When did I get so damned old?

I stand, planting my feet firmly on the ground. I don't want to indicate that I'm tipsy, even to Moreno. The man would never let me live it down.

I shove my hand into my pants pocket to retrieve my keys.

Nope, not there.

I check my other pocket. My wallet is there but no car keys.

Exhaling a heavy breath through my nose, I head back toward the booth I had occupied earlier with the raven-haired treat.

There's no sign of my keys on the booth or under the table.

"Looking for something, boss?" Moreno asks. He stands behind me and is wearing a grin.

Is this some sort of joke? "Did I give my keys to you already?"

I swear I'm not that trashed. Just a little tipsy. But fuck, the room spins like a carnival ride when I bend down.

Moreno isn't smiling or joking. He doesn't look amused.

"The girl, she stole them from you."

"Nicole?" I run a hand through my short dark hair.

No. She wouldn't steal from me. Anyone with half a brain knows not to cross the Ricci Family.

But she didn't know I was Don Ricci, the boss of the Ricci Family.

"Dante, how about I make a call and get one of the guys to bring us a car?" Moreno suggests.

I wave him off to do whatever he needs to while I scuttle toward the door. I step outside and the night has cooled down quite a bit. It's summer, hot and oppressive, but the chill in the air makes me long for the cooler days that will come soon enough.

One of the advantages of being in the mountains, the nights are quite comfortable.

I don't see my truck outside, not that I expect she left it. If Nicole stole my keys, then she stole my truck.

Surprisingly, she left my wallet alone.

Was it a game to her?

Did she know who I was when we met and played me?

————

I rise early thanks to a shitty night's sleep.

Moreno knew not to say a word about the truck while Sawyer picked us up and drove us back to the house.

I tossed and turned, unable to get a decent shut-eye because of that raven-haired beauty, Nicole.

She was all I could think about last night.

She is still all that I can think about.

But I have work, and as much as destroying her father and stealing her for myself sounds promising, I have a business to handle.

I stumble into the bathroom. I flip on the light and start the shower.

There's a commotion downstairs—more than usual.

I ignore it. Whatever or whoever it is can wait while I clean up for a handful of meetings I have later this afternoon.

Business doesn't wait, even for the boss.

But business doesn't show up early.

Could it be Nicole? Would she come to return my truck?

I'm quick to bathe and shut off the shower. I shouldn't be thinking about her, but I can't stop the memories that flood through my mind and fill my senses.

My cock hardens, remembering her clenching down and shuddering in my embrace.

She shouldn't have this effect on me. I've slept with my share of women. I can get any woman I want, but there's something about Nicole that makes me itch for another play with her.

I dry off and run a towel through my hair to get the last water droplets out when there's a hard knock on my bedroom door.

Could it be her?

"Boss," Moreno says and clears his throat. "Sheriff Nelson is here to see you."

I wrap a towel around my waist and open the bedroom door to speak to Moreno in private.

What did the sheriff want with me? We'd been careful to keep our business dealings above board since Enzo went and got himself executed.

I killed him.

It had to be done. He was bringing down the family and ruining the Ricci name. His involvement with human trafficking still brings bile to my mouth.

I'm a man of many talents and business dealings. I've sold drugs, illegal weapons, you name it, I've dabbled in it, but I won't stand for such inhumane behavior as selling women and children.

It's another reason that I intend to destroy the DeLuca Family. As far as I'm concerned, they're the reason I was forced to kill Enzo.

"Any idea what he wants?" I ask. I gesture for him to shut the bedroom door.

He closes the door behind himself.

I grab clothes from my dresser and closet and take the articles into the bathroom. I leave the door open so that we can speak privately.

What I'm really asking if his visit is because of Enzo's disappearance. We made sure there was no body to be recovered, but that doesn't mean the feds and the local sheriff's department aren't going to dig around looking for dirt.

"Something about your truck," Moreno says.

I can't see him while I dress, but I can feel the concern that ebbs off him and flows to me.

"Then we'll take care of it," I say.

We can handle whatever drama that Nicole throws on our doorstep.

I zip my slacks and button my dress shirt, making sure I look like the boss. I can't have the local sheriff looking down on me.

I have a reputation to uphold.

And uphold it, I will.

"Let's get this over with," I say and gesture for Moreno to open the bedroom door and step out first.

He leads me down the stairs and to the living room where our guest is waiting.

Sheriff Nelson doesn't sit. He stands, one hand on his weapon. He appears anxious, though I'm not sure why.

We've kept our dealings to ourselves and have done our best not to warrant unwanted attention from the authorities.

I don't need my men getting sent to prison. That doesn't bode well for me.

"Mr. Ricci," Sheriff Nelson says.

"Dante," I offer, correcting him, letting this become a familiar and friendly visit, trying to change and shift his mannerisms. I want to allude to him that we are friends and that he has nothing to fear being in my home. The first way to do this is by letting him use my first name.

"Dante," Sheriff Nelson says. He gives a flick of a nod. "We have surveillance footage of your truck stealing fuel from a gas station. I've spoken with the owner, and knowing that you're an upstanding citizen in this community, he's agreed not to press charges if you drive down and pay for this little mistake."

Moreno opens his mouth to speak, and I shoot him a glare. He's not about to interrupt me.

No one interrupts me.

He lowers his voice. "Now I saw the footage. I know it wasn't you. If you'd prefer to hand over the name of the girl who did this, I'd be happy to arrest her and book her."

"That isn't necessary," I say.

Why am I covering for Nicole DeLuca?

I could have her ass tossed in prison.

I should have her facing the consequences of her actions, especially after stealing my truck, but turning her over to the authorities isn't how we Riccis do things.

No, we take justice into our own hands.

She'll pay for her crimes, but not at the hand of the local sheriff's office. "I assure you, Sheriff, I'll handle the matter right now."

I grab my wallet and another set of car keys. She stole my truck, but at least she didn't lift the Maserati.

"I'm sure you understand that I have to follow you to the gas station," Sheriff Nelson says.

"Of course, I'd expect nothing less of you."

————

I'm fuming when I return home to the compound.

I can't believe that Nicole not only stole my truck but also decided on her little joy ride to forego paying for gas.

Was she trying to get arrested?

Maybe I should have told the authorities who nabbed my truck, but it wasn't like I couldn't afford it.

The same could be said for her. She is the daughter of Gino DeLuca.

The girl is easily worth a million, maybe two. When her father dies, she stands to inherit his empire.

Another reason that I need to destroy Gino and keep an eye on Nicole. I'm not going to let her become the next don.

Abso-fucking-lutely not.

"Everything handled, boss?" Moreno asks as I storm into the house.

"I want surveillance on the DeLuca property. I want to know everything that's happening in that house regarding Nicole."

Moreno glances at his cousin Halsey, a capo. He is still relatively new to the business and young.

It was the fact he was fresh off the block that DeLuca wouldn't recognize him.

"I've got connections locally," Halsey says. "We can interrupt his internet feed and force him to call the cable company."

"Do it." I wave my hand, indicating that he is dismissed.

I motion toward the empty hallway where Halsey just exited. "Do you think he can handle it?" I ask.

I trust Moreno. He recommended Halsey to run the soldiers and give orders. I'm not sure if he is capo material, but this is an excellent opportunity, and we need to seize the moment.

If he fucks it up, I won't have to kill him. DeLuca will do it for me.

4

NICOLE

I abandon the truck on the side of the road, not far from the house. Bringing the truck home would just infuriate Papa and have him questioning where I've been and what I've done.

The damned tank was near empty, so I filled it up at the nearest station.

I planned to run, but I couldn't get far without a place to sleep.

No credit card, and if I had brought mine with me, Papa could easily have it traced.

No cash.

I wasn't going to sleep in the back of the truck.

Home sweet home, my prison.

But I'm allowed to come and go as I please. Although Papa insisted I bring a guard with me, he didn't seem to care that I ran off last night.

I sneak inside well after midnight.

Papa is asleep, and the guards don't appear all that surprised to see me.

I slip inside the house. The door squeaks behind me.

He isn't waiting for me. Did he even realize I ran off?

I hadn't been exactly quiet about it. More and more, his focus has been on being don. It's all that matters to him and I get in the way.

I climb up the staircase and tiptoe into my bedroom. I feel like a teenager all over again, sneaking out and back in past curfew.

————

I avoid Papa as best I can.

He's in a hellacious mood, screaming at his men, his colleagues.

I can hear him from my bedroom with the door shut.

My stomach gurgles, but I don't want to face his wrath when he's already terrifying to be around. I had forgotten what it was like not to feel that heavy weight of anxiety pressing down on my chest.

Going away to college had been the best thing for me.

Returning home had been my private hell.

Why had I done that?

Oh, right. I didn't have any money but Papa's. Every cent that I had earned while in college had been spent on my housing, food, and transportation. I'd gone to Northwestern, not a cheap school, and Papa had paid for the tuition without batting an eye.

I sit at the edge of my bed. I shouldn't still be thinking about the man from last night, the one at the bar.

I'd stolen his truck.

That had been out of necessity, not want. And if I ever saw him again, he'd probably hate me.

It didn't matter. I wasn't planning on sticking around Breckenridge for long. I had two options, find a way to siphon money from Papa or get a job.

The first would be more difficult, but there had to be cash lying around his office.

I open the bedroom door. The hinges creak, and I stand there like a doe in headlights waiting to see if I'm about to be Papa's next victim.

"What do you mean his truck is just outside our front gates?" Papa screams at Marco from down the hall.

Marco is a few years older than me, but he wears his age well. He's tall and brooding with a thick head of luscious jet-black hair.

Sometimes I want to run my fingers through it, but I don't get the impression that he's interested in me.

Is it because Papa is his boss?

It's a game.

Toeing the line of what is and isn't allowed.

I've kissed him in the back of the hall closet and given him a blow job in the kitchen before everyone was awake.

That was when I had been in high school, and he'd pushed me down onto my knees, demanding I do as he said.

My stomach somersaults at the memory.

Four years away from the castle, and I'm a different girl. I'm no longer Nicole. I'm Nikki.

Nicole would never have stolen the truck.

Maybe four years wasn't long enough to rid my identity. I'm no different from the men downstairs. Stealing. Thieving.

Although I haven't murdered anyone yet.

I can't say the same about Marco. And I know Papa has killed many men in his day. I've witnessed the brutal atrocities in the dungeon where I didn't belong.

"And get the damned internet up and running!" Papa shouts.

"I've already called the cable company. They are sending someone out this morning," Marco says.

Since when did he get promoted to errand boy?

I sneak past the yelling and screaming and hurry with light, invisible footsteps to the kitchen.

My stomach grumbles, and I think it might give my position away, but no one seems to notice or care.

————

After breakfast, I pack a bag and grab my backpack, slinging it over one shoulder. I take it with me to Papa's office.

Papa is still having a heated conversation with Marco, and this time Vance, his second, has joined in whatever discussions they are having.

I hear bits and pieces as I walk by. "War... turf... Ricci."

Some things never change. The DeLuca and Ricci family have always been at war with one another for as long as I can remember.

Doesn't matter the city or the year. The war continues.

I sneak into Papa's office and slip inside when I see a boy who doesn't even look old enough to drink standing on a step stool messing with the drop-down ceiling.

He clears his throat. "Almost done here, ma'am."

My eyes scour over his outfit. His shirt identifies the cable company that he works for, and he appears genuinely nervous.

"The router appears to have short-circuited. I've replaced it with our newest model that gets better range than the previous edition and wired it through the ceiling to get—"

"Whatever," I say and cut him off.

I don't give a rat's ass. I want him out of Papa's office so that I can snoop around and find his hidden cash supply.

He smiles politely, climbs down from the step stool, folds it up, and leans it against the wall before letting himself out of the office.

Well, that was fast.

I wait to make sure he doesn't return and then hurry to the desk. I search the drawers, but there are papers and scribbles of notes. Nothing worthwhile.

Heading for the filing cabinet, I yank one drawer open and then the second.

Jackpot!

Inside a manila folder is several thousand dollars. The money is crisp and wrapped like it was picked up at the bank. I drop several wads of cash into my bag and zip it up.

I shut the drawer in a hurry just as the office door swings open.

"Nicole?" Papa's brow furrows. He gestures to the chair, ignoring or not noticing the bag over my shoulder.

Knowing Papa, he's probably ignoring it. He has a knack for detail.

"Sit." It's a command that rolls right off his tongue. He points to the empty seat across from his desk.

I know I can't run.

He has too many men who can stop me.

Hopefully, he won't ask to see what's in my backpack. It's mostly clothes, a few staples of food, the truck keys, and now several thousand in cash.

5

DANTE

"We've got the microphone up and running. I couldn't finish getting a camera in place," Halsey says over the phone. "Some young girl walked in and nearly ruined the operation."

He just left their compound.

"One other thing, boss. Gino and his men were arguing about your truck. I passed it on my way over."

"My truck?" I try not to sound too surprised. "Where the hell is it?"

So much for that. I can't stop the anger that broods out of me, like a lion in a cage ready to spring free.

Halsey pauses for a second before answering my question. "You parked it right near the gate, about two clicks south."

"Of course, I did," I mutter. What the hell was Nicole thinking?

Was she trying to get me killed? Did the DeLucas think I was scouting their property?

Halsey is lucky he's not dead.

I hang up the call with the young capo and gesture for Moreno to hurry the hell up. I'm not great with patience or waiting.

Moreno pulls up the audio surveillance. I don't expect much, but we give it a listen.

"I'm tired of your selfish games and your attitude, Nicole. You are just like your mother," Gino says. His tone is firm and filled with discontent.

"Are we done?" Nicole asks.

I smile at the sound of her voice.

I shouldn't. I should be angry with her for stealing from me, but that is a mess to deal with another day.

"Hardly. I was serious about the marriage arrangement. It isn't a choice, Nicole. You are my daughter, and I will marry you off to the man I deem acceptable."

"I'm not a prize to be won at the state fair," Nicole says. "I'm leaving and you can't stop me."

Silence fills the void.

I glance at Moreno. "I really wish we had video."

It's probably the selfish part of me wanting to see Nicole again. But I can still see her, feel her nestled tight against my cock.

She was tight, virgin tight, with that tiny little hole that I fucked.

God, I want her.

Inwardly, I groan and bolt for my office. I need a few minutes. Silence. A moment to myself.

I still have my phone in my hand, and Moreno installed the program so that I can hear Gino anytime he's in his office.

I leave it on, waiting to see if Nicole storms back to give him the last word.

She seems the type.

"Shut the door," Gino says.

I don't know who he's speaking with, but the authority in his voice is commanding.

"My daughter is a problem that needs fixing."

That piques my curiosity and my interest.

She is a problem. My problem.

I don't know what Gino's issue is with Nicole. While I'm not fond of the idea of anyone choosing another's spouse, I understand the notion. Our family has had arranged marriages for centuries. It's the way we do things.

My father's marriage was an arrangement between families. They both seemed happy. Mostly.

"Yes, boss," a male voice says. It's rough and thick. Not the least bit young or new. He speaks with authority, like he's comfortable with Gino.

I know it's not Vance, Gino's second. I'd recognize his voice with my eyes shut.

"Nicole is going to run. The child is pissed at me, and I'm not going to stop her. She stole several thousand dollars from me. I want her captured by our operation. Our men aren't to know that she is my daughter."

"But, sir—"

"No!" Gino's voice bellows. "This is for her own good. She needs to discover what it's like to be sold to a monster."

My blood boils. The room is hot like a sauna, and sweat drips from my forehead. I wipe it away.

I loosen the top three buttons on my shirt and slam my fist into the wall. My knuckles burn, and my fist tingles, but it does nothing to dull the ache in my chest.

Gino is the monster, and Nicole has no idea what is coming.

6

NICOLE

I toss the backpack over my shoulder, lace on my favorite pair of sky-blue sneakers, and head for the front door.

Papa doesn't so much as look my way.

He doesn't care that I run. I'm just an annoyance to him.

Outside, the sun is blinding and warm. I stroll past the guards on the lawn for the gate.

"Do you need a ride?" one of the guards asks me.

"No, that's all right. I'll walk." I fully intend on digging out the keys to the truck once I'm past the gate and out of sight.

The gate squeaks open with a shrilling rattle that sends a shiver down my spine. I ignore it.

There are more men standing guard than usual.

Papa was angry this morning. Did he worry that we were in the middle of another turf war? I'd heard bits and pieces and wasn't an idiot.

Papa and the Riccis don't get along. Never did. Never would.

I stroll through the open gate. I nod my thanks to the guards and keep my sights ahead on the bend in the main road. That's where I parked the truck.

It wasn't out of sight. It had been late when I'd come home, but I doubt anyone thought anything of it. Vehicles break down all the time, and it was just before the private road that led to the house.

I reach the truck and drop my bag on the ground. I need my keys, and I don't have them handy.

Well, Daniel's keys. I crouch down and unzip the backpack. My fingers sift through the contents, pushing the wads of cash aside first, and then fiddling through my clothes.

I should have left the keys in the outside pocket. That would have been smart, but I wasn't thinking this morning.

Papa always makes me nervous.

My hands tremble. I exhale a heavy breath and turn around just as I feel a bag going over my head and my hands being thrust behind my back.

Cuffs dig into my flesh.

He doesn't identify himself. It's not a police officer.

"Who are you?" My question goes unanswered.

Strong arms lift me, and the roar of another vehicle's engine hisses and thuds.

"Let me go!" I squirm and shriek, doing my best to fight, but my arms are secure behind me, and I don't have a chance without a bit of help.

"Do you know who I am? You can't do this! I'm Nicole DeLuca. My father will kill you!" I scream at the men abducting me.

They shove me into the back of a vehicle. It's lower to the ground.

I'm not in the truck that I'd stolen.

Where were they taking me?

They ignore my pleas, my screams, my shouts for help.

Is this because I stole that hottie's truck last night? Was he teaching me a lesson?

Strong arms come closer. I can't see much but light and shadows through the blackened hood.

Hands lift the hood slightly around my neck. Are they removing it?

Instead, I feel the cold leather of a collar, and the buckle is yanked tight—metal prongs inside dig into my neck.

I wince and groan from the discomfort.

"Shut up!" a thick voice bellows out at me.

A jolt of electricity zaps me.

I'm trembling. Shaking. Convulsing.

I'm not sure if I was tasered or electrocuted through the collar. Is there even a difference?

The current stops, but my body still burns and aches. My neck is sore. My throat hurts inside my mouth.

I don't fight back.

I hang my head. I'm a coward and give in to the men. Whatever they want, I will give to them.

Anything to never feel that pulsating burn through my body.

7

DANTE

"You aren't seriously considering getting involved?" Moreno is standing with his arms crossed.

He doesn't look the least bit amused.

"The way I see it," Moreno says, "this solves a problem."

I shake my head. "No." I may be a monster, but I have a conscience. I don't sell women or children. I've spent several months as head of the Ricci Family by working to destroy the DeLucas.

The easiest method is through their human trafficking operation.

My motives aren't entirely selfless.

I want to destroy Gino.

I don't know what I will do with Nicole if I lay eyes on her. My head can't wrap around how to handle this problem.

I'm too emotionally invested.

Moreno sees it too. He knows me almost as well as I know myself.

It would be risky, waltzing in—possibly a suicide mission—to save a girl who stole from me.

"I have contacts. But you might be better equipped to locate the address of the auction," Moreno says.

I've burned bridges.

I can't just up and call an old colleague, an associate who now works for the enemy. He's as much a cop to me as he is private security.

I swallow back the bile at the thought of associating with Jayden Scott.

"He works for Eagle Tactical," I say, and my top lips snarl with disgust. Those men took down Angelo DeLuca when Angelo had been don.

In a way, they'd done me a favor. It also led to my decision to execute Enzo. It was him or me.

He'd have pinned his entire smuggling operation on me.

I wasn't going to let that happen. It's why I've been careful.

Eagle Tactical also went after Sergio, Angelo's capo. As far as I know, they killed him or maybe the girls he'd taken had. I wasn't sure which and didn't care.

Except Sergio was no longer hosting the auction. I don't know where the operation will be running from.

Only when.

It's always midnight.

————

I shouldn't do this.

But what other choice do I have?

I leave the compound and drive toward the headquarters for Eagle Tactical. Those guys aren't going to be happy to see me.

I park at the end of the driveway and walk toward the building. Pulling out my phone, I text Jayden Scott.

I need a favor.

I don't like doing favors because it means I'll owe him one. But he should be thrilled to help me. Those Eagle Tactical guys are practically like the Boy Scouts with their code of honor and shit.

My phone lights up with a response.

Fuck off.

I smile and laugh under my breath. I can't do that, or rather, I won't.

Come outside and say it to my face.

I don't stand right in front of the door. I'm off to the side, my arms folded across my chest. I'm taking a gamble he won't come out here with a loaded pistol and shoot me.

We haven't exactly been on the best terms lately. Enzo nabbed his fiancée and handed her over to the DeLucas.

Enzo hadn't given me much warning of the situation, and when I told him I was against it, he told me to shut the fuck up.

So, I did.

I knew where I stood. I wasn't boss then. Now I am.

Now I make the fucking orders.

The front door swings open, and Jayden steps out. His eyes are tight, and his hands are bunched into fists.

Thankfully he isn't brandishing a gun, and if he does have one, it's put away, concealed.

I'm okay with that.

It's not like I go anywhere without my weapon secured to my hip and a spare at my ankle.

My insurance policy.

"Some nerve you have coming here!" Jayden shouts at me.

I expect to see watchful eyes in the window, but it's too hard to tell if anyone is staring at us or not.

"I know. Trust me. You're not the first call I wanted to make, either." This isn't ideal for either one of us.

As far as I'm concerned, we betrayed him, and he crossed us. It should all be behind us. Somehow, I don't think he feels that way with the steam radiating off of him.

Actually, I'm not sure he betrayed us. I have suspicions, and he certainly invited a rat into our home. This means he's either an asshole or an idiot.

He lunges at me, but I dodge the first blow and grab his arm, pinning it behind him while my other arm squeezes down on his neck.

"That's enough!"

The front door swings open, and Jaxson Monroe is in full haste, coming at me. "Let him go!"

I toss Jayden at Jaxson. "I'm not here for a fight."

"Could have fooled me," Jaxson says. His eyes flinch, and his bottom lip is tight, unwavering. Tattoos cover his forearms. Not a surprise for a guy who served in the military. "What do you want?" he asks.

"Gino DeLuca, does that name mean anything to you?" I ask.

Of course, it does. He'd be an idiot not to know the second of the man he took out. He did me a favor, cutting off the head of the snake. Well, figuratively, of course.

"I'm not cleaning up your mess. Whatever feud going between the DeLucas and Riccis, we're staying out of it," Jaxson says. He gestures for Jayden to get inside the office.

Jaxson is the one in charge.

Interesting.

I knew Jayden was new to joining the security team. He had worked for me before his involvement with his former military buddies. I should never have trusted him, and here I was again, making the same mistake.

"DeLuca's still trafficking women. Possibly children." I have no evidence that he's trafficking kids, but I know for a fact his daughter was tied up in that mess, and if I can get to Jaxson, pull at his heartstrings and play with his emotions, then maybe he'll get me the intel that I need.

Jaxson's right hand balls into a tight fist at his side. His left runs a hand through his hair. I've seen that look before from many men, my men even. He's conflicted.

"What do you care? Aren't you mafia thugs all the same?" Jaxson steps closer.

He isn't afraid of me.

But he should be.

"I'm no saint, but I don't think women should be forced into sexual servitude. Do you not agree with me?" I ask.

Of course, he agrees with me. He's one of the good guys. Or at least he pretends to be. He probably has his demons, the same as the rest of us.

No one is truly a saint.

"Well?" I ask, waiting for his answer.

"What do you want, Dante?" Jaxson folds his arms defensively against his chest. He hasn't stepped any closer, but he also hasn't turned to go back into the office and slam the door in my face.

I'd consider it a win so far.

"I have it on good authority that Jayden attended one of these soirees. I need the location."

Jaxson laughs under his breath. "You are insane. Do you know that?"

"I've been told." I shrug. That doesn't make me want the information any less. "Well? Can you help me or not?"

I'm trying the nice guy approach—reasoning with an intelligent man and full of something I don't have, ethics.

It seems to work.

"Sergio was the one who ran the last auction, but he's not up to the task of handling it anymore," I say.

Sergio is dead.

I have it on good authority that the Eagle Tactical guys took care of his ass. He was a scumbag, forcing women to do countless sexual acts.

I'm a different kind of filth. Sergio and I, we're not cut from the same cloth.

"Do you have an address?" I ask. I don't want to appear desperate, but let's face it, I wouldn't be coming to these guys if I had the information.

Could my men procure it?

Yes, but it would take time.

Time was something I didn't have much of, considering Nicole was in trouble.

Why do I think about her?

She is a distraction. And it is becoming a problem.

Men like Jaxson and Jayden tiptoed on the side of the law. I'll bet they've probably expunged a few records and erased a few parking tickets too.

"Seems Jayden has your number. He'll text you with whatever we find," Jaxson says.

Good. I try not to seem overly excited.

"Don't ever come back here," Jaxson says as he turns for the steps up to the entrance of the building. "Or I'll make sure to put a bullet in your head before you can so much as knock on the front door."

8

NICOLE

The compound is stuffy and stale. The air doesn't circulate, and it's hot as Hades.

It's dark, and the floor is even warm, although it's made of concrete. There are bars that keep us contained, made of iron and rusted.

The smell first burned my nose when I arrived, but now I've gotten used to it. We're given a bucket to piss in, and once a day, a guard comes to retrieve the metal bin and empty the contents.

The only food we're given is bread and water. I scarf every bite before the guards can think twice about snatching it back from me.

Would they do that? They certainly don't seem to care about us. They can't even look at us.

I've been here for three weeks.

Or maybe it's four.

There's no sunlight. We're kept in some type of cellar. We all arrived with bags on our heads and collars around our necks.

The bag comes off.

The collar always stays on.

I can't speak unless spoken to.

That's one of the rules. There are dozens more, but mostly keep your head down and do as you're told.

Diamond has a long list of them, and if you cross her, disobey her, or just look at her the wrong way, I've learned that the collar around my neck sends a jolt of electricity barreling through me.

It turns out the other girls are linked to the same network.

If one of us does anything to betray Diamond or the men who took us, we all suffer together.

Today is different, and I'm not sure why. It scares me.

The girls don't know who is behind their abductions.

Seven of them came up from Mexico and were promised passage into America. Coyotes.

Four girls are runaways. They barely look like they're in high school.

They're young children, and it makes my stomach roil. I want to vomit but it doesn't come up.

The girls clutch each other as the men unlock the gate and rip us out one by one.

Where are they taking us?

What do they want with us?

We know better than to ask questions. Asking is met with revolting pain that makes us thrash wildly on the concrete floor.

The collars are a death sentence. Or maybe just being here will bring about death. Our death.

I want to fight.

There's no fight left in me.

The other girls must feel the same. Dejected. Destroyed. Broken.

One foot moves in front of the other.

There are more men with guns, and we are dragged from the prison cell and led up the concrete stairs.

The steps are chipped and broken. Old and worn.

Where are we?

Where are we going?

I'm in the middle of the line, and the younger girls are in the back. If we could protect the youngest, we would, but we are all prisoners here.

Men with guns stand at the top of the stairs. They're grinning. What do they know that we don't?

They lead us outside. The sunlight feels wonderful and warm. I want to run, but there are a dozen guards with guns.

We are outmatched and outnumbered.

The moment the door shuts behind us, the weapons are pointed at us.

"Strip!" one of the guards commands.

No one undresses.

The collar electrifies, and my fingers grip my neck. I can't remove it. It's instinctual, but it doesn't help settle the pain.

I'm on the ground—the dirt at my bare feet.

Twitching and trembling.

Pain is my only friend.

I hate this life.

A blast of cold water assaults all of my senses.

I scream and realize the chill feels good. It takes a moment to comprehend what the hell is going on.

"Strip!" the guard commands again.

Beside me, the girls all glance at each other and slowly, methodically, we disrobe.

There are no houses as far as the eye can see. The land is flat. We're in the valley somewhere.

Which means we're not in Breckenridge. At least, I don't think we are, but I'm not sure.

The hose of the spray pounds against my bare skin.

The sun is hot and fierce. The spray feels good once I get used to the fact men are staring at us naked.

I want to scream at them. Shout that they're all a bunch of sick assholes, but I know if I do that, the collar will burn my neck and hurt not only me but the other girls.

Four of them are still children. I don't look their way. I can't.

It's cruel.

Sickening.

I want to vomit, but all I do is tremble and gasp for air.

As quick as the spray hits us, it's done. The shower is over, if you can call it that.

The guards lead us back inside. I glance over my shoulder at the outside world and the towering metal gates surrounding the property.

Even if I wanted to run and manage not to get shot, the collar is still on my neck, and the fence would be a bitch.

"Move!" the guard who sprayed us bellows out.

We trample through the building. We're given a towel to dry off and clean our feet. They don't want mud and dirt tracked through the house.

Ironic.

We're led around the inside of the building on the first floor. It's old and still smells musty. I'm grateful they're not shucking us back into the basement prison.

There's blue and white damask wallpaper on the walls. The carpet is plush but worn.

It reminds me of an old folks' home. Worn. Forgotten.

Who lives here?

"Move!" one of the guards barks. He shoves the barrel of his gun at me.

I tremble—my heart races.

He laughs, his eyes glint with excitement, and it makes my stomach flop.

Does he know who I am?

Is that why I've been taken? Did the Riccis abduct me? I don't know what Dante Ricci looks like, but I suspect he's behind my kidnapping and imprisonment.

Who else would be such a monster?

Surely, if they are looking for ransom, Papa will pay for my freedom. Won't he?

Or is this a message to hurt my papa?

The girls in front of me shiver and wrap their arms around themselves. The air is still stale, but it's strangely cooler on the first floor.

Maybe it's the fact we're all soaked.

The towels are snatched away.

We're naked and at their mercy.

The ceiling fans are on high, buzzing and whipping about. It feels good against my skin.

"Girls!" Diamond's voice permeates the room. "This way!" She leads the parade. I see her now, wearing a red sequined dress that hugs every inch of her body. She's got a dynamite figure.

It almost makes me jealous.

Right now, I'm only jealous that she's in control and commanding us to obey.

Diamond leads us into a small room. The windows are open, but metal bars have been welded to the inside. There's no escaping.

The door slams shut behind the last girl who enters.

A lock clicks into place.

The same game, another place.

We are their prisoners.

———

My eyes flutter open in a haze. I've been drugged. I can still feel the effects of the injection humming through my body.

I rub the back of my spine where the needle pierced my skin. That was after they dressed us, did our hair, and made us playthings.

But for who?

I'm dressed in a thin, pale pink negligee, and I wrap my arms instinctively around myself. The clothes are see-through and leave little to the imagination.

I wear nothing underneath and sit up.

The room is dark except for the tiny light overhead.

I'm on display.

But for who?

Through my foggy gaze, I spot another girl being harassed by a man in a suit. He's forcing her to sit on his lap, and his fingers run through her bright red hair.

My stomach flops. I stand. I can't watch this anymore and not do something.

As soon as I stand, my legs give out from under me. The plush velvet of the booth I've been situated in cushions my fall. It's not the same location where I'd been held at gunpoint.

My fingers graze over the collar. It's still there.

Why did I think it would be gone?

I cringe as I stand again, determined to protect the other girls. The truth is that I need just as much protection and saving. Won't Papa come and rescue me?

The spots before my eyes fade, and I pull my legs up beside me in the velvet booth.

Men are filtering into the darkened room. It's hard to see them, but my eyes are adjusting to the darkness. Or maybe whatever they've given me is beginning to wear off.

I see him before I even realize I'm trying to stand. I want to gesture him over to help me, save me, and protect me. But then I realize he's just like the rest of them.

Shame envelops me and burns right through my core. Daniel. He works for the Ricci Family. It's the only assumption that I can make, and that's why I'm here as a prisoner.

From my seat, I watch the confrontation between Daniel and his men. I can't hear the words exchanged, but they look heated. They also have a gun pointed at him.

It seems he's pissed off some important people.

I feel less bad about stealing his truck now that I know he works for a monster: Dante Ricci.

Shouts and shoves, heated words are tossed back and forth between the men.

Daniel really pissed someone off. I sigh, trying to watch the heated argument, when Rafael heads over toward me.

Is he my saving grace?

"Rafael?" He works for Papa. He must be here to save me.

"Zip it," Rafael commands. "Your father will be here soon, and he's already disappointed in you. Don't disappoint him further."

What?

He turns on his heel and grabs a drink off a waitress who's coming around with shots of something. I wish I could have one to dull the pain and go back to that hazy state that I was in earlier.

The women who wander around carrying trays of liquor are wearing short, dark blue sequined dresses. They all wear the same gown. I'm pretty sure if they bend over, I'd get an eyeful of their assets.

At the sight of Papa, my eyes light up, and I wave at him, hoping that he's come to take down the Ricci Family once and for all.

"Papa!" I shout across the room.

He's sharply dressed, and a cigar bobs from his lips. He pulls it out long enough to throw a punch at Daniel.

They exchange heated words before Papa storms across the room and through a distant hallway. I can no longer see him.

Did he not hear my scream?

Tears well in my eyes. The makeup will indeed be smeared, and I pry at the collar, wanting the wretched leather and metal off me. I gasp for breath, certain that I'm choking and the collar is strangling me.

Heavy sets of footsteps approach. "Deal with her," a man in a suit says to the other men.

Are they talking about me?

Daniel whips out a hundred-dollar bill. "Give me an hour with her," he says.

He'd been positioned behind the other men in suits who had approached. I hadn't seen him at first.

Maybe I didn't want to see him.

Rafael plucks the money from his fingers. "Four hundred for twenty minutes." He holds out his hand, expecting the additional funds deposited into his palm.

Daniel retrieves his wallet from his pocket and pulls out a wad of crisp hundreds. "An hour," he reaffirms that he's buying me for the next hour.

Why is Rafael collecting the money? Is he working for the Riccis?

Where did Daniel get that money from? How much more does he have in his wallet?

Maybe I should have snatched his wallet instead of his truck keys. It was too late now to second guess the past.

The other men disperse, and Daniel is left standing over me, looming and brooding.

He looks pissed. He also has a shiner on his cheek. The guys roughed him up.

I still don't understand what is going on. Why were Papa and Rafael here?

I want to run. The intensity of his stare, his tight eyes, and how he threw money at Rafael makes me nervous.

What does he intend to do with me?

I push myself up from the velvet booth, my legs still wobbly, but I begin to stand. Maybe I can skirt him and make a run for the exit.

If only I knew where the exit was located, and I wasn't wearing that stupid collar.

"Sit." His harsh words cause a shiver to course through my body.

He looks angry with me. It's probably because I stole his truck. Who the hell is he? How did he have so much money?

The capos did well for themselves, but they weren't tossing money around the way Daniel had to buy my time.

I shiver. What was he going to do to me for stealing from him?

If he is with the Ricci family, then I am in serious trouble.

"Daniel," I whisper.

How can I not be surprised to see him? I try to soften my voice and make myself sound less of a vixen than I am.

"It's Dante," he says, correcting me. "Dante Ricci."

9

DANTE

It'd been hell trying to get into the party. The DeLucas didn't want me to attend the soiree, and while I didn't have an invitation, I was hoping they'd be accepting of a little green.

Boy, was I wrong. Their soldier guarding the entrance had recognized me the moment I stepped foot inside.

With a gun poised at the back of my head, he alerted Rafael of my presence, which brought out Gino to give me a word of warning to leave.

The problem is that I don't take direction very well.

Especially from a thug like Gino.

After mincing words and getting a few blows to my face and chest, the boys opted to let me stick around to take my dough.

One look at her in that sheer pink ensemble, and my cock hardens.

Fuck.

I don't want to think about her. Not like this, and certainly not now.

She looks sheepish and concerned that I might betray her. She has no idea what I'm capable of and what I've done.

Around her neck is a collar. It's leather at the edges and metal in the center. I've seen something similar used to control prisoners and imagine it's a torture device of some type.

I almost feel bad for her.

Almost.

She stole from me.

No one steals from Don Ricci. Ever.

She made me look like a fool in front of my second, Moreno. Thankfully, he kept what happened to himself, and we never spoke of it again. Well, almost never.

Does she know the police showed up at my door?

She brought the fucking cops to my house!

"Sit down," I command her.

There isn't anywhere for her to run or flee. Dozens of DeLuca's men control the facility. My men are on standby outside of the perimeter, in case I don't come out alive. They have their orders.

She shivers like she's cold. It's impossible not to let my gaze rake over her body. Her rosy nipples are hard and puckered through the thin, flimsy fabric.

I don't want to stare. I have no desire to be like the men here, wanting a taste of flesh for a few dollars.

I've never needed to pay for sex. And these women aren't prostitutes; that would imply there was consent on their part.

They were prisoners.

"Daniel." Nicole's soft whisper and long eyelashes bat up at me as she sits back down in the booth.

I try not to let my head grow cloudy with memories of the last time we were in a booth together. Her body writhing above mine, clenching onto my hardened cock.

The room feels several degrees warmer. Did they crank the heat in this place?

"It's Dante," I say. My gaze never wavers or falters. "Dante Ricci."

She deserves to know the name of the man who intends to buy her. I've paid for twenty minutes with her, but I fully intend to take her home with me, whatever the cost.

Her eyes are wide, like a doe, and I take the opportunity to sit beside her. I rest a hand on her thigh, and she freezes and holds her breath.

I don't want to be the monster that I am. She knows my name. She's terrified of me and for a good reason, but does she realize how awful her father is and what he was willing to do to teach her a lesson?

Now isn't the time. There are likely cameras and audio surveillance.

I have to tread carefully. This may be a suicide mission, saving her, but I don't intend to end up dead.

"Why are you doing this?" she stammers.

I frown, confused by her question. With a heavy sigh, I realize she probably has no idea that I'm here to save her.

I'm not the animal keeping women locked up in cages.

I grab her chin and force her to stare into my icy gaze.

We aren't alone. DeLuca's men could quickly snatch her from my clutches if they so much as desire to punish me.

To say I'm surprised her father, the head of the DeLuca family, the don, hasn't stopped me from laying my hands on his daughter is an even more disturbing thought.

What kind of man would not protect his daughter?

His flesh and blood?

"I will own you, Kitten," I say.

She swallows and tightens her lips, rolling them inward.

Does she have nothing to say to me? Even after she stole my truck?

Her gaze glances past me. She's probably looking for help, but no one will come and save her.

I'm all she has. I'm her knight, but I'm not here to ride away off into the sunset together. I will take her with me, bring her to my castle, and protect her from her father, even if it means locking her away like Rapunzel.

Her voice comes out as a squeak, soft and unsure of herself. "I'm not one to be owned," she says.

"You're mine," I rasp and plant my lips forcefully on hers, reminding her of that night together when we were two strangers and didn't know the truth.

Well, she was the one who didn't know. I plucked her like the delicate flower she is, and now I will crush her.

The daughter of my enemy is mine.

10

NICOLE

I shouldn't want to be his, Dante Ricci's, but the way he takes command brings me back to that night together, the two of us at the bar.

Did he know who I was that night when we met?

I flinch as he grabs me, takes authority, and reminds me that I am nothing without him.

Just a plaything.

That's all these men think of me as, a sex object.

It disgusts me.

He plunges his lips on mine and I bite him. The bastard had it coming.

I taste the metallic zing of blood. I pierced his lip. Nothing trivial.

Dante pulls back from the kiss, brings his thumb to swipe his lip, and unveils the damage that I've done.

I'm expecting him to slap me, choke me, maybe even kill me.

A jolt of current hits me from the collar around my neck. My punishment sends my body to the floor of the bench. I'm clenching my neck, jaw tight, and teeth grinding together.

"Enough!" Dante bellows out into the room.

The pain dulls, but the electricity is done, for now.

I blink back watery eyes. Did the other girls suffer because of what I did? I'm too afraid to glance around the room and discover that I'm to blame.

He pulls me onto his lap.

"I paid good money for you," Dante says. His voice is loud, like he's bragging that I'm his prize for the time being.

What's he trying to prove?

His breath tickles my ear as he leans in and brushes the wayward strands of hair behind my ear. I shiver from his touch.

Does he notice?

My stomach flops at his breath. It's warm and inviting.

"Kitten, look around," he says, and with his hand on my jaw, he slowly turns my head.

I glance around the room. The girls are giving lap dances or blow jobs. Even two of them are fucking the men, riding them like stallions. It's all out in the open. There's not even a semblance of privacy.

What does he expect me to do? I refuse to get on my knees for him or fuck him.

I didn't know who he was at the bar when we met. Now that I know he's an animal, I won't give in to his demands.

"No," I say, staring at him. "You got your lay from me at the bar. I won't fuck you ever again." If I had known who he was, I wouldn't have touched him.

Was this the price that I paid for that act? Perhaps it was because I stole his truck.

"You will," Dante says. "But not here. Not tonight." His eyes are dark but shine with mirth as he crushes my lips and pulls me onto his lap.

It's his fault that I'm here. I'm certain of it. This is his club.

I hate him for it, the abduction, the humiliation, the way his men treat the other girls and me. Some of them children.

"I'll never fuck you again," I say, my words dripping with venom.

He cocks a sly grin. "Never is a long time, Kitten."

I hate the nickname that he's given me. It's sweet and playful.

Dante isn't either of those things.

He's watching me but distracted.

Every so often, he glimpses past me at the men, but his hands are on my hips, firm.

I glance in the direction that he keeps focusing his attention on, but I don't see anyone. It's dark, and there are shadows everywhere. Silhouettes of men as they roam around the large, dimly lit room.

Is he looking for someone?

"You're a monster. Abducting women and children to parade them around and sell them for a few minutes of fun. It's repulsive."

He opens his mouth but shuts it.

"Cat got your tongue?" Disbelief overpowers him. "Yeah, that's what I thought."

I've rendered him speechless.

"I could ruin you and your father. Demolish the entire empire that he's created," Dante says.

I try to suppress a shiver that courses through my body involuntarily at his words. "Go ahead and try," I say, bold and daring him to make his move.

Papa wouldn't let anything happen to me, right?

In the darkness, there are several sets of eyes observing us. We are being watched. Is it Papa or Dante's men?

"Why me?" I ask.

Dante refuses to answer my question.

His fingers glide from my hips to the hem of the gown and graze my bottom.

I inhale sharply at his touch. These men expect something.

Dante is no different.

Dozens of questions are reeling through my head, but all I've earned is his silence.

Is this all because of his truck that I stole?

His fingers graze my neck, and he tugs my head to the side, allowing him better access.

The tips of his fingers scratch my throat. He's gentle, not anything like I'd imagine Dante Ricci, the don of the Ricci family, to be. I'm waiting for him to choke me, hurt me, kill me.

Something is wrong.

He's wrong. Off.

I stare into his black eyes like two stones of coal, and I feel drawn in, taken heart, body, and soul.

What is it about him?

His lips descend hard and rough on my mouth. He has one hand on my jaw, positioning how he wants me, holding me, claiming me.

This time I don't bite him.

I give in to the darkness and temptation.

My lips part and I grant him access.

I shouldn't want this. I should hate him.

I do hate him.

Despise him, in fact, but he's Dante Ricci, and he gets whatever he wants.

What he wants is me.

His fingers trail a rough path over my hip, and I lift myself just enough to let him touch me if he so dares.

I want this. For the first time in days, I feel alive and there's a spark of hope. But I'm conflicted that Dante is the one bringing me that light in the darkness.

Hate burns through me, and his hand wanders teasingly along my thighs and up towards my aching center.

He doesn't give me what I want.

Why should he?

Dante paid for his pleasure, not mine.

His hands roughly push my hips back down on his lap. He's forceful and not the least bit gentle. Dante's breath caresses my neck as he whispers into my ear, "Don't you dare come, Kitten."

11

DANTE

My time is up. An hour whizzed by and I'm reminded that she isn't mine to have for another minute.

"I'll buy her now, outright for the entire night," I say.

There's a look of desperation behind her amber eyes. She can't beg me to stay, but if she could, she would be on her hands and knees right now.

I've teased her, and that's all I've required her to do for me.

Any other man would have forced her to give him a blow job and shoved their hardened cock down her throat until she choked.

I can see the fear behind those golden flecks of honey, and her hand is clenched on my thigh. Her fingernails are sharp. I'm surprised none of the men have cuts from her fighting back.

Nicole seems like a fighter, and something tells me the fire hasn't been extinguished from within her yet.

I pat her thigh and guide her from my lap to the booth. The material is crushed velvet. It's soft and probably caresses her naked backside.

Desperately, I want to feel her slit, discover the sheen of glistening desire that pools between her thighs. It is, after all, only for me.

The men at this soiree are vile and disgusting creatures.

I feel like filth just being here.

But I can't let my focus change.

I have to protect Nicole. If not for her, then for the Ricci Family. She is my bargaining chip.

After I put her onto the booth, I climb out, wanting to have a word with DeLuca's men. I gesture for her to stay.

"No one touches her," I demand.

The big guy, who is not so much tall as he is wide, indicates for his bosses to come over. Rafael slums over.

"You again?" Rafael says. "What now?" He doesn't even pretend to look happy to see me.

Why should he? We're enemies.

"How much to buy the raven outright?" I say.

I point to Nicole. We're far enough away that she can't hear our conversation. That's how it must be.

I pretend not to know that she's Don DeLuca's daughter, or that I even know her name. It's better if they think I don't care.

Except I can't fool them when I'm demanding no one else can get their claws on her.

Rafael snorts indignation. "You're insane. She's not for sale. Unless you plan on marrying her, buyers can choose their bride for a steep price. We like to think of it as matchmaking. We help facilitate the arrangement of marriages." He smiles a toothless grin. "The IRS has fewer problems with it too. We're a dating service."

My stomach flops at the disgust for Rafael and the men who run this place.

Was Gino DeLuca actually considering selling his daughter to a man for marriage?

Fuck.

It doesn't matter the cost. I won't let anyone else take her home.

She is mine.

"Will one hundred thousand cover it?" While I don't have that kind of cash just lying around, I can easily wire them the funds in cryptocurrency. I'm sure they won't object.

"Let me talk to the boss."

"You do that." I fold my arms across my chest and wait for Rafael to return.

Gino steps out from the shadows.

How long has he been hidden in the darkness of the room? I hadn't seen him. Had he been watching me with his daughter?

His nostrils flare as he steps closer. He's a few inches shorter but stockier.

Gino's also old enough to be my father. His face is pockmarked, his eyes a deep-set brown, and his hair thick but obviously dyed. His bushy eyebrows are salt and pepper, while his hair is as dark as the room. He blends in with the shadows.

He gestures me closer and lowers his voice.

This conversation is between just the two of us. His men can't hear us, and neither can Nicole.

"Do you know who she is?" Gino asks. He turns his head to squint in the direction of his daughter. "She is my blood."

"I offered your man one hundred thousand for her. Why bring her here if you don't intend to sell her off?" I ask.

His jaw is tight and crooked as he grinds his teeth.

Did I say something to piss him off?

I know why she's here. It's to teach her a lesson. He's pissed. This is his way of controlling her.

It is sick and fucked up.

I may be a monster, but I'm not an animal. Not like him.

Gino clears his throat. He doesn't even so much as glance at his daughter. "For double, you can have her, but you should know that she's betrothed. Her husband-to-be will come looking for her. The only way to sever that alliance is if you intend to marry her."

I swallow the lump in my throat.

Marriage?

Gino has to be fucking with me.

"You want me to marry your daughter?"

There has to be a catch.

Is Gino trying to get information about my family and my men? Would he use Nicole to gather intelligence?

I have no intention of marrying, ever. Relationships are a distraction and a weakness.

Sex involved no strings or complications, nothing that would detract from my responsibilities to the family and the business.

And while I had wanted to ruin Nicole and destroy Gino, marrying her seemed a far more complicated issue than a solution.

"Consider this a token of my gratitude that you remain out of this business. And let it be known that I never want to see you or your men at my party, ever again," Gino snarls.

It still doesn't add up. I can't believe it is really about the money, not with his daughter.

"One other thing," Gino says. He gestures me to lean closer.

I'm hesitant, but I don't think he'll kill me now, especially when he had his opportunity earlier when I showed up at the event.

"My daughter is never to know that I was behind her abduction and this club. If you tell her, I'll kill both of you myself. Now, do we have a deal?"

I can live with the notion that she'll think I'm behind her kidnapping and that I'm the monster. At least she'll be safe. I'm saving one girl tonight.

12

NICOLE

Dante escorts me off the premises and into his nearby vehicle. Needless to say, it isn't his truck.

With a firm grip on my forearm, he opens the door and shoves me inside.

I stumble into the sports car. It smells new and looks clean and shiny from the outside.

Did he buy it today because I stole his truck? Or was this vehicle sitting around untouched because he's a rich bastard with too much money to his name?

Honestly, I'm terrified of the man. I don't want to go with him, but there never seems to be a choice. At least not for me.

Dante crouches down and leans into the car. He grabs the seatbelt and reaches across my lap, securing it in place.

"I don't want anything to happen to my precious cargo," he says.

"I'm not a piece of luggage," I snap.

He pulls back and slams the door shut on the passenger side.

Dante hurries around and lets himself in. There's only enough room for the two of us in the car. He must have ridden alone.

"Your men won't miss you?"

I'm met with silence.

I glance back at the brick building with dozens of vehicles parked out front. My fingers graze over my neck, and I exhale a heavy, jubilant sigh. The collar is gone.

Dante removed the thick leather collar from around my neck and left the device on the booth.

I can finally breathe.

But I'm not free.

At least not yet.

Dante slams on the gas and the vehicle jars forward, tires spinning and kicking up dust and dirt. I don't have to ask where he's taking me.

I already suspect that it's to his home, his private lair. But I don't know where that is exactly. Somewhere in town, I suspect.

He keeps his hands to himself on the drive.

Every so often, I feel his stern gaze shoot at me. How much more torture will I have to endure because I stole his truck?

The vehicle whips around curves as we travel up the mountain. There's grass to my right. If I can just roll out of the car, maybe I can escape as long as I don't plummet down the ditch.

It has to be a better fate.

I yank the handle for the door, and it opens.

Dante thrusts out an arm to grab me and hold me back while he slams on the brakes and lifts the emergency brake.

We come to a hard halt.

We both reach for the buckle.

Dante tries to stop me, but my hands are tiny, and with the door already open, I have an advantage.

I unclasp the buckle and dive out of the open car for the forest.

It's only seconds later that I hear him chase after me.

"Nicole!" he shouts, and the sound of his shoes crunch against the gravel.

I skid down into the ditch, doing my best to keep my footing, but it's steeper than originally intended.

I lose my footing and trip over my feet, rolling, tumbling, and falling several feet until I slam into something rough and sharp.

My head throbs, my stomach aches, and I'm seeing double.

I push myself up to stand, but Dante is on me before I can get up.

"You're not going anywhere without me," he says and scoops me up into his arms.

I want to fight him and scream.

My pleas are soft, tiny, and practically non-existent.

Can he hear me begging for help?

I mumble incoherently as he carries me back to his car and sits me down in the passenger seat.

Dante emits a heavy sigh. "You can't make this easy, can you?" he asks.

I don't know what he's talking about.

My vision swims.

He's opening the glove box and yanks my arms behind my back. I feel the icy cold metal of handcuffs dig into my flesh.

"You're wearing these until you can be trusted," Dante says.

He slams the car door shut.

There's no way to escape. I am at his mercy.

13

DANTE

The brat couldn't chill and keep calm on the car ride over to the complex. I didn't expect she'd be thrilled to come with me, but escaping took serious balls.

I don't trust her to tell her my plan. All I intended was to buy her freedom, keep her away from her psychotic father, and then drive her to the nearest bus station.

She still wore that sheer pink negligee. Gino hadn't even handed the girl a robe to change into.

Nicole needed clothes. We can stop at my place, find her something suitable to wear, and then I can have one of my men drive her out of town.

That had been my plan until she opened the car door and fled on foot.

Maybe I shouldn't have chased her. But what was I to do, let her return home?

It will get us both killed.

I need to get her back to the complex, clean and bandage her wounds. Hopefully, she doesn't have a concussion.

"Stay awake," I command.

Her eyelids flutter open, and she groans. I can't tell if she's making sounds because she feels sick or it's a result of falling down the mountainside.

I doubt she'd tell me the truth if I asked her.

And those handcuffs are a bitch to wear. I almost feel bad, but I can't take a chance that she'll try to escape again.

Every few seconds, I glance at her out of the corner of my eye, and I careen the rest of the way up the mountainside to my place.

It's secluded, off the beaten path, and a hideaway.

It's less formal and flashy than my predecessor's compound.

I don't need to draw attention to myself or the family, especially from the authorities. They've been keeping a watchful eye and waiting for us to slip up.

I'm not an idiot. I have enemies who would turn over anything they could to put our family out of business.

Bringing Nicole to my home is a risk. I should drop her off at the bus station with a one-way ticket to the east coast, and I will, but she's injured and tired.

I have men who can take care of her, a doctor who can ensure she's healthy before sending her on her way.

Tomorrow, I'll never have to see her again.

It's just one night with her at my house. How much trouble can one girl cause?

14

NICOLE

"Can you please remove the handcuffs? I swear I won't try to run again," I say.

He doesn't answer me.

We pull up out in front of Dante's home.

It's beautiful from the outside, old and large. I'm surprised it's a log cabin, but it's huge. It easily stretches on for two properties in a typical residential area.

However, he doesn't live in a city or suburbia.

We are out in the wilderness. Dante probably owns hundreds, if not thousands, of acres.

The windows are dark but made of glass that goes from floor to ceiling along the road-facing entrance.

It is serene and peaceful and offers a false sense of security.

There is nothing peaceful or calm about Dante.

He kidnapped me, bought me, and has now handcuffed me as he drags me inside his home.

Does he plan on parading me around in front of his staff?

Dante leads me out from the car, his hand around my arm as he guides me up the steps and around the wrap-around porch to the entrance.

"What's downstairs?" I ask as he unlocks the door.

Dante exhales a sigh and flips on the light. He pulls me inside the house and turns me around while he disarms and then resets the alarm, not letting me see the code.

The same man I saw Dante with at the bar that night strolls over toward us. He has a crooked nose, something that I hadn't noticed earlier from a distance. He smiles warmly at the two of us.

"Boss."

"What is it, Moreno?" Dante asks, his tone clipped. He sounds every bit like how I feel, tired, exhausted, and ready to sleep for the next century.

Dante shoves me at Moreno. "Take her upstairs, show her the guest quarters. I'm going to call the doctor and see if I can have him drive out tonight."

"Tonight?" Moreno asks, glancing at the clock on the wall.

"Yes. She took a nasty spill, and I want to make sure she's all right," he says. "I'll call from my office. Make sure that she has everything she needs for the evening."

My hands are still bound behind my back. It's uncomfortable, to say the least, and after stumbling down the mountainside, my shoulder is a bit tender too. I have a few bumps and bruises, but my vision is better than it was earlier.

"Of course, boss," Moreno says.

Dante tears off down the hallway, and I'm whisked up another staircase.

"This way," Moreno says. He takes my arm to guide me up the steps and down the long hallway. To the left, is a balcony that overlooks the entryway. To the right, door after door is shut.

Past the balcony, there are four additional doors on the left. Moreno opens the second one on the left and leads me inside.

Once inside, he retrieves a set of keys and gestures for me to turn around.

I breathe a sigh of relief when he unclasps the handcuffs that Dante put around my wrists. While the collar had been far worse, the cuffs weren't exactly pleasant, either.

"Thank you," I say and pull my arms around in front of me. I rub at the red marks and grimace.

Moreno frowns but doesn't say anything. He steps across the room and opens the adjoining door. "The bathroom is through this door. There are clean towels hanging on the hook against the wall if you'd like to clean up before bed."

I do want to shower, to rid myself of the filth that covers my body, but I'm afraid that Dante might decide to accompany me in bed.

If I'm disgusting, he won't want to join me. Right?

"Are you hungry? Would you like me to have the staff fix you something to eat?"

I shake my head no and grimace. The movement roils my stomach. I hurry for the bathroom, toss open the lid of the toilet and expel the contents inside. There isn't much to bring up except bread and water.

Moreno backs out of the room and I hear the lock click on the door.

I flush the toilet, rinse my mouth with water, and then stalk out of the bathroom. I try the handle to the bedroom door, but it doesn't budge.

He's locked me inside.

Wonderful.

From one cage to another. It's all the same, just a different prison.

————

I'm tired and dirty. I don't bother showering. I climb under the covers and flip off the bedside light.

Just when I think I might actually fall asleep, there's a loud, forceful knock at the door, and the lock clicks.

Dante flips the wall switch, and the overhead fan light brightens the bedroom.

I squint and shield my eyes as I sit up.

"What is it that couldn't wait until morning?" I'm grumpy when I'm tired, and it has been days since I slept through the night, let alone in a warm and cozy bed.

At least, this prison, I could get used to. Not that I want to, but it is comfortable.

Is this some form of torture or interrogation method? Is he intentionally depriving me of sleep?

"Doctor Blake Reiss is here to examine you after the nasty spill you had this evening," Dante says.

I don't correct Dante. He probably has the doctor in his pocket and they're friends.

"I'll wait outside," Dante says and heads for the door.

"Wait!" I'm not sure why I stop him from leaving. While I don't trust Dante, I trust this doctor even less.

Dante's brow furrows as he steps farther into the room and approaches the bed.

I inhale a sharp, nervous breath. My breathing hitches just slightly, and he comes to sit at the edge of the mattress beside me. "I'll stay here the entire time if that would make you more comfortable, but I can assure you that Dr. Reiss is an upstanding physician. He'll take good care of you, Nicole."

It's the first time he's said my name tonight. At the club, I was kitten to him.

My breath catches in my throat with a slight sob. I'm emotional, a wreck, and definitely overtired. Tears blur my vision. "I prefer Nikki," I say, correcting him.

"Of course," Dante says. He gently rests a hand on my leg, which is buried under the blanket.

The doctor steps closer and brings out a penlight, checking my pupils, my vision, and then my reflexes. I can't tell if he's concerned or just a blank slate. He gives no indication whether everything is all good or if I'm dying.

"And you've been throwing up?" Dr. Reiss asks. "When was your last period?"

I shoot a glare at Dante. His colleague Moreno must have told him that I had vomited earlier.

"I don't know. I've never been very regular."

The doctor opens up his medical bag and retrieves a pregnancy test. "You should take this in the bathroom."

I stare at the box.

"I hit my head," I say.

It can't be possible that I'm pregnant. Can it?

Dante and I had sex but I don't feel pregnant. I'm not exhibiting any other symptoms as far as I can tell.

"Yes, but you were also vomiting. It's just a precautionary measure. I'm sure it's just a mild concussion," Dr. Reiss says. He stands. "I'll give you two a minute. I'll be just outside the door."

I continue to stare at the pregnancy box.

No.

I won't do it. If there's even the slightest chance that I'm pregnant with Dante's kid, I don't know what he will do or how he'll react.

I'll fake the test. Dip it in water instead of urine.

I don't think that I'm pregnant, but I sure as hell can't take the chance it will come back positive.

Dr. Reiss shuts the door as he leaves the bedroom.

With a heavy sigh, I stand up from the mattress and patter off toward the bathroom, pregnancy box in hand. I try not to make a big deal about it.

"Leave the bathroom door open," Dante says.

"What? Why?" I glance over my shoulder at him.

Dante's brow tightens, and he lunges off the mattress, following me to the bathroom. "Until I can trust you, I need to see you take the pregnancy test myself."

I snort under my breath. "Are you worried I don't know how to take a pregnancy test? It's not rocket science."

"I'm worried you'll lie to me."

"I'll let you see the stick," I say.

Dante shakes his head. "Yes, and you'll probably stick it in water or drop it in the toilet bowl to dilute it. I don't trust you."

15

DANTE

She spins around on her heel and shoves the pregnancy box at my chest.

"And you think that I trust you?" Nikki scoffs at me. "I swear to God that if I'm pregnant, I'll terminate it."

"Excuse me?" My voice thunders at her suggestion. "The hell you will!"

I may not have wanted a kid, but there is no chance in hell that I am going to let her threaten to end the pregnancy.

Grabbing her wrists, I back her up into the bathroom, trapping her.

The stupid box with the pregnancy test falls to the floor. I kick it with my foot, bringing it with me into the bathroom.

"Get off of me!" Nikki shouts, struggling against me.

I'm tired of her antics. It's clear that she's used to getting what she wants. Maybe I should have expected it, considering who her father is. "Control yourself!"

I slam the bathroom door shut behind us and the walls vibrate.

She squirms against my grip until I finally let her go.

With a sigh, I bend down and hand her the box, letting her unravel the contents inside and take the test. I'm not sure whether she needs the instructions that accompany the test or not.

"Will you at least turn around so I can pee in private?" Nikki asks.

"No." I fold my arms across my chest and lean against the shut door.

It's not like her clothes aren't already revealing.

There were t-shirts and sweats in the drawers of the bedroom. She hadn't showered, let alone changed clothes before she climbed under the covers. With her thin pink negligee, I can see everything.

Nikki grabs a disposable cup beside the sink for water and sits on the toilet. She takes the pregnancy test, and although I don't stare at her, I watch to make sure that she isn't cheating me of the truth.

She flushes the toilet and washes her hands. The cup with the pregnancy stick sits on the bathroom counter. Nikki purses her lips and sits down on the edge of the bathtub, her hands on her lap, shaking her head.

Her complexion has turned ghastly. Is she nervous about the results or still not feeling well from earlier?

I'd been stupid not to use a condom. I've always been careful for this very reason. I am not ready to be a father.

I glance at my watch, keeping an eye on the time, waiting to check the test.

The absolute worst-case scenario stares back at me —two pink lines.

Pregnant.

16

NICOLE

No. No. No.

That damn pregnancy test must be wrong.

I blink once, twice, and stare at the two lines on the pregnancy test that don't seem to vanish.

My vision had been blurred earlier. Was there even a tiny chance that I was the only one seeing that I was pregnant?

One glance up at Dante and I take a step back.

He will never let me go. Not while I carry his child.

"So, it's settled," Dante says. He clears his throat, and his eyes flinch before he turns and storms out of the bathroom.

What is settled? I fold my arms protectively against my chest.

My head hurts and my stomach is somersaulting from the news.

I can hear his muffled voice just outside the open bathroom door. Anger resonates through his tone. Even if I want to ignore him, and I desperately do, his voice is loud and booming.

He's in the hallway speaking with the physician.

I toss the pregnancy test into the trash and wash my hands. One glance at my reflection in the mirror and I don't recognize the girl staring back at me.

I slam the bathroom door shut. Of course, there's no lock. There's nothing to shove in front of the bathroom door to keep it secure except for the stupid little trash can that holds the pregnancy test and the box. There's nothing else in the mint green can that matches the towels hanging on hooks.

I storm toward the shower and turn the knobs, blasting a jet of hot water into the tub. The shower pours down as I strip and toss my clothes on the floor.

The curtain is fabric, with hints of blue, green, and gold in horizontal lines. I yank back the cloth material and step under the hot spray.

The water feels good, unlike the last time I had been blasted with a hose. I shut my eyes and tilt my head back. The roar of the shower drowns out Dante and the doctor.

Perfect.

It's just what I need.

I lather my hair with shampoo. The fragrance is sweet and energizing with hints of spearmint and lavender. I rinse the suds and am relieved to find a bottle of matching conditioner.

These aren't manly fragrances, and they don't smell at all like Dante. Does he usually bring women home from the bar or the trafficking operation?

A shiver burns through me.

How many women has he owned?

I reach for the shower and crank the heat all the way up.

I know the shower isn't cold, but I'm trembling and my teeth chatter.

I finish washing up as quickly as I can and shut off the shower spray. I pull back the curtain for a towel and stare into Dante's sharp gaze.

"Get out!" I point at the door. "Who the hell told you that you could come in here?"

Dante hands me a towel from the hook. He's silent.

"I could have found that myself." It wasn't like I had to dig around for a towel. The linens had been left out.

"I thought I'd give you a hand."

I yank hard, pulling the towel from his grasp and wrap it around myself.

"When I want a hand, I'll ask for it," I snap. "Why are you still in here?"

Has the man no understanding of privacy?

"We need to talk," Dante says. He takes a step back but stands in the doorway, his arms above his head as he leans on the molding.

He irritates me. I reach for the bathroom door to slam it shut.

Dante's eyes flinch, but he stops the door from closing on him.

"Moreno!" he shouts.

"What? Do you need to invite your entire crew up here to see me in the shower?"

"Technically, you're getting dressed," Dante says. His demeanor is cool and calm, collected.

It's not the least bit like how I'm feeling. He's gotten me into a frenzy, knocking me up and now this, invading my personal space.

"I'm not dressing with you staring at me," I bite back. There's no way Dante is getting another opportunity to gape at me naked. Not if I can help it.

I keep the mint towel positioned tight around my body. One hand clutches the material while I attempt to fend off Dante with the other.

"Out!" I command.

My orders do little good.

Dante cracks a sideways grin. His gaze is filled with amusement and a spark of something that I don't recognize. Is it mirth?

He blocks me from leaving the bathroom, and even if I wanted to dress, any clothes that are tucked inside the dresser drawers are behind him.

Is this some type of game to him?

There's a firm, resounding knock at the bedroom door.

"Come in," Dante says.

"Seriously? Have you no regard for anyone else's feelings?" I ask.

I pull the towel tight. Not that Dante can see anything, but now with another member of the Ricci family inside my bedroom, I'm even more vulnerable and exposed.

"Sir," Moreno says and clears his throat.

Dante takes a step back from the doorframe that he's been blocking. "I want the pins removed and this door taken down."

"What?" I gasp. He has to be crazy.

"My wife thinks she can give me orders," Dante says with a dark laugh. "It's time she learns what it means to be married to a don."

Wife?

Married?

"You're insane," I say. "There's no way that I'd ever marry a monster."

17

DANTE

I hadn't intended to tell her about the marriage without sitting her down, and certainly not while she was dripping wet and clutching a towel to her chest.

The towel barely fit around her cute, curvy body.

She aggravates me and when I get irritated, I tend to lash out.

Bad habits are hard to break.

I order Moreno to remove the pins along with the bathroom door. If she is going to be difficult and slam the door in my face, two can play at that game.

Besides, Nikki needs to know who is in control.

And it isn't her.

"You're insane," she fires venomously at me. "There's no way that I'd ever marry a monster."

She isn't wrong, and I don't cower to her names or her bullying.

Nikki is tough. She's had to be, growing up with a father like Gino. Anything less, and I'd think she is holding back.

"Do you honestly believe that you have a choice?" I step toward her and feel the sizzle of electricity in the air between us. The hum vibrates, and she leans in toward me.

Does she even realize this small gesture tells me that she wants me?

She opens her mouth to retort, but quickly shuts it. "We're having a child together. It doesn't mean we have to be anything." Nikki gestures between us. "This, what we had, one stupid night, is over. It will never happen again."

She says that now, but she'll change her mind.

I can see it in those deep amber gems that sparkle every time she lays eyes on me. I'm certain her pulse is throbbing in her neck. That's probably not the only place that it's throbbing.

I gaze down at her body. The damned towel is still clutched in her grip.

Nikki can think she's won this round as I take a step back into the bedroom.

My heart races every time I glance her away. Passion isn't love. I don't fool myself into believing that I could ever love anyone.

But that doesn't mean I'm not a man fueled with desires.

"Her door, remove it at once," I say and point at the bathroom door. It isn't a question. Moreno takes orders from me.

Moreno gives a sharp nod of agreement. "On it, boss," he says and hustles out of the bedroom to retrieve a hammer and large screwdriver.

Nikki skirts past me as quickly as she can. I grab her wrist and pin her against the wall.

One hand grasps her towel, and the other is poised above her head, trapping her between the wall and me.

"Dante, what are you doing?" she whispers, staring up at me.

Her lips part and she emits a soft breath that pulls me nearer.

I swear I hear her purr.

"Claiming you, Kitten," I say. "From this day forward, until that baby is born, you will remain here under my protection."

Nikki struggles against my grip, fighting me.

"You'll never have this baby—my baby," she snarls up at me.

"Is that so?" I stare down at her. She has no idea the things I did to rescue her and buy her safety.

Even if I wanted to let her leave, now that she's pregnant, I can't.

Nikki harbors the heir to the Ricci throne if it's a boy. If it's a girl, she will still be my flesh and blood. I refuse to deny either the Ricci name.

"You can't keep me here against my will," Nikki says.

"It's for your safety. Besides, as far as I'm concerned, you haven't repaid your debt."

The color drains from her face. Her eyes widen and sparkle. "About that," Nikki says. "I can explain."

"Don't. Anyone who steals from a Ricci ends up dead at my hand or with a few digits cut off."

She swallows nervously, her jaw tight. Nikki no longer fights me, which gives me the opportunity to bring her other hand up to the wall above her head.

"Dante," she whispers, her brow tight as her towel falls to the floor.

I should stop myself before I lose all control. Moreno will return any minute, not that I care what he sees.

My lips fall to Nikki's neck, and she emits a soft purr from the back of her throat.

It grows louder as my soft kisses arouse her.

Yes, that was definitely a purr. She moans and shifts her legs apart just a little. She's no longer tight and buttoned-up, clenching and keeping me at arm's length.

"We will never be more than co-parents," I say, mimicking her desires.

"Mm, yes, that's right," Nikki mumbles in agreement.

I kiss a warm path across her neck and down toward her breast. With one hand, I keep her hands above her head. With the other, I let my fingers wander over her peak, teasing her nipple before bending down to suck and taste, kiss, and lick her.

Her head dips back and her eyes are slammed shut.

She's enjoying this almost as much as I am.

"You will be mine," I say as I let my fingers skim down and across her stomach.

Her hips rock forward. It's obvious what she wants. Do I give it to her?

She moans, and her breathing deepens as my fingers graze her hip. All I do is tease her, let my touch wander, and excite her.

"Say it," I command.

She's quiet for a moment. It's the first time that I think I've rendered her speechless. "Say what?" she asks.

"That I am yours to do with as I please."

Her eyes lazily open. She's breathing hard and heavy. Her cheeks are flushed, and the same matching blush has spread across her chest. "No," she pants. "Never."

I release my grip, take a step back, and leave her bedroom. I shut the door with a loud thud behind me.

Moreno stands outside in the hallway. He is clearly waiting to go inside, tools in hand. "I, uh, just took a minute to find the hammer," he says and quirks a grin.

"Wait until morning," I say. "No one goes in or out of that room until tomorrow morning." I grab the key from my pocket and secure the bedroom door, making sure that she's not able to escape.

She's pregnant with my kin. There is no chance that she is getting out of here without one of my men or me at her side. I can't take the chance that she'll run to a clinic and get our little problem fixed.

Nikki is having that baby, and if she doesn't want to be a mother, she can leave the minute my child is born.

18

NICOLE

What the hell was that? Why did I let him seduce me? It has to be the hormones. But I'm only a few weeks pregnant.

Is that even possible?

I retrieve a perfectly crisp and clean black t-shirt that rests above my thighs. It's long enough to cover my bottom and intimate areas. I curl under the sheets and sleep for what feels like a week.

By morning, Moreno is waking me, insisting that I get up and start my day.

"Go away," I mumble as he stands over my bed.

"It's noon. You've already slept the day away," Moreno says. He yanks open the curtains, and sunlight pours into the room.

I shield my eyes with my arm.

"I've brought you clothes, and once you're dressed, you may come with me downstairs to the kitchen."

Sitting up in bed, I pull the covers up around my waist. "You'll let me out of this room?" I ask. I was certain after last night, Dante would never let me leave, that I'd be locked away in his castle forever.

"You can come down for breakfast, yes." Moreno gestures to shopping bags on the floor beside the dresser. "I wasn't sure what size you were, so I bought one of everything this morning."

There are dozens of shopping bags filled to the brim with new clothes, the price tags poking out. The clothes are from a variety of stores, each bag from a different shop, none of which are located in Breckenridge.

He must have gone out early and started shopping the moment the stores opened.

"You weren't joking," I say.

I'm reluctant to climb out of bed until he leaves the room. I don't have pants on, let alone panties. The shirt does cover me, but not enough as far as I'm concerned.

Moreno smiles. Does he sense my hesitancy? "How about I give you a few minutes to search through the clothes and then come back to lead you down to the kitchen?"

"I can meet you downstairs," I say. Although I don't know where the kitchen is located, I'm sure that I can find it.

Moreno offers a curt nod. "I'll wait outside your door." He steps out of the room and shuts the door behind him.

I suppose he doesn't trust me.

Why would he?

After a few seconds alone, I climb out of bed and saunter toward the dresser, where there are several large bags filled with clothes, folded and neat.

I rub the sleep from my eyes and turn the plastic bags upside down, leaving the clothes on the floor. I grab a pair of jeans in my size and a t-shirt, along with panties and a bra.

My stomach flops knowing that Moreno bought me undergarments. Most of the items are sensible but the bras and panties aren't the least bit plain or nude. They're a variety of colors, sizes, and styles. Everything from thongs and bikini bottoms, and push up bras to lacy sheer cups from the finest designers.

Dante definitely has money.

I spend no time getting dressed and run my fingers through my tangled hair. It will have to suffice. I patter to the door and turn the handle, surprised to find it unlocked.

Moreno stands on the opposite side, waiting for me.

"Are you hungry?" he asks.

The thought of food doesn't excite me, but I also haven't eaten much in days. Shouldn't I be hungry?

"Come with me," he says when I don't answer.

I follow him down the hall and then the stairwell to the main floor. We wind around the inside of the house until we reach the kitchen.

Inside, there's a high-top table with four chairs. No one else is seated, but already, there's a plate with food, a glass of milk, water, and orange juice in front of the place seating.

"No elegant dining room?" I joke.

"I thought you might find this a little more comfortable and familiar," Moreno says.

Did he forget that I grew up with Gino DeLuca? He does know who my father is, doesn't he?

"Will anyone be joining us?" I ask.

What I really want to know is if Dante will be having breakfast with me or if he's avoiding me.

"No, Dante is away on business for the next few days."

"Oh," I say. I'm not sure why I care. I should be relieved that I don't have to see him. Not dealing with him sounds quite enjoyable.

Moreno seems nice, friendly, and maybe I can convince him to let me go from my imprisonment with Dante.

"Does everything appear to your liking?" Moreno asks.

He's formal, far more so than the men who Papa dealt with. Moreno has kind eyes and a warm smile, but I know behind his façade he'd murder a man without thinking twice.

"Yes, I'm just not that hungry." I climb onto the chair and sit in front of the enormous amounts of food.

It feels wrong to have all this when the other girls are starving. What happened to them? Is that why Dante is gone?

Is he snatching the next runaway or filling his compound with girls to be sold at auction?

I push the plate away. "I'm not hungry," I say.

Any appetite I had is long since gone.

"You need to eat breakfast. If not for you, for the baby you're carrying," Moreno says. His voice is soft yet firm. I'd guess if Dante was here, he'd force me to eat.

I should be grateful that he's been called away on business, but a small part of me is sad not to see him.

He stirs a fire within my very soul. I'm not sure whether I should hate him or be grateful he plucked me away from Diamond and the other men who could have easily had their way with me.

I sigh and reach for the glass of juice. "Can I ask you something?" I glance at Moreno.

He's standing guard by the door. I'm not sure what he's waiting for, worried that if I run, he'll have to chase me? His boss probably wouldn't be too happy if I got away. Good.

Moreno shrugs.

"How many other girls has Dante brought here? How many women has he caged?" I ask. I'm honestly not sure that I want to know the answer, but at least then I might come to terms with my fate.

It doesn't sound like he has any other children, and if that is the case, at least Dante has a reason to keep me around and keep me alive.

Moreno clears his throat. He shifts his feet a bit. He looks more than just uncomfortable. He seems downright afraid to answer me.

What have I gotten myself into?

19

DANTE

Avoiding Nikki isn't hard, especially when I'm handling business. I need to feel in control, and the fact she's having my child makes me more uncertain about everything.

Including her.

Nikki getting pregnant shot my plan to Hell. I had every intention of shoving her onto a bus, giving her a hundred dollars, and sending her on her way.

That was the plan.

The plan changed.

Staring at that stupid pregnancy test made me realize one thing: I wasn't going to let her leave.

I spend four days in Chicago rubbing elbows with the Russians. I return home and head straight for the shower.

I feel like the filth I've been hanging around.

Gino is the enemy I know. The man is not the least bit spontaneous. He will continue to traffic girls until he's dead, and even then, I'm not sure I can stop him. There are too many heads to bring down, too many men who would gladly sit atop his throne.

The thing of it is, betrayal isn't a hard bargain to strike. I know that.

Gino certainly knows that.

I'm not an idiot. Sending one of my own men in undercover would get my man killed.

Sending anyone from Breckenridge would be a suicide mission.

Our town is too small.

The Russians and I have an understanding, an agreement that we keep off each other's turf, and we are willing to help one another on an absolutely necessary basis: life or death.

I've asked for their help. I'm still awaiting their answer.

Their empire is built on infiltrating organizations, hacking into companies, holding business secrets for ransom.

I need their expertise with the DeLuca empire to bring them down. Whether it involves holding their assets hostage or turning over their secrets to the Feds to destroy Gino and his men, I'm not above rubbing elbows with the Russians.

Exhaling a heavy breath, I slam the front door behind myself and storm up the stairs for that shower. I need to rid myself of the blood and sweat that sticks to my skin.

In a matter of minutes, I'm standing under the spray, and the hot water leaves a trail of red where it's touched. I should turn the tap down, but I don't.

I won't.

A cold gust of air sweeps through the bathroom. On the opposite side of the glass, there's movement.

"Whatever it is, Moreno, can't it wait?" I shout, assuming he's the ass interrupting my five minutes to myself. Who else would be dumb enough to storm into my bathroom?

I need this time to myself to unwind.

The glass door slides open.

"Nikki?" I blink twice and rub the water from my eyes.

How the hell did she get out of her room? I haven't slept much the last few nights in a hotel, but this doesn't seem real.

"Your stupid bodyguard Moreno won't let me leave," Nikki says. Her cheeks are red, and her pouty bottom lip juts out as she stands there, waiting for what, exactly?

I'm not going to let her waltz off with my child.

"Seems like you found your way out of your room."

I don't know how she did it. Did she pick the damned lock from the inside, or had the younger guard, Leone, forgotten to lock her inside her bedroom? He'll be reprimanded later for his mistake.

"And you had to interrupt me in the shower to tell me that?"

"No."

I'm not used to being thrown by a curve. Not like this. She doesn't get to make the rules and play games with me.

I'm the one who is in charge.

"Get in here," I growl and pull her under the hot spray.

She shrieks, and I'm not sure if it's because it was unexpected or the fact she's still fully dressed.

"Dante!" Her jaw hangs agape. She seems mystified that I just soaked her.

Nikki has no idea what she's in for.

How wet I intend to make her.

"What did you expect?" I back her up against the cold bathroom wall.

She shivers.

My fingers pull at the hem of her white t-shirt, which is now revealing her purple bra. Thank you, Moreno!

I rip the shirt from her body, tearing it down the center, and toss the soaking remnants on the floor. It puddles.

"What are you—" She doesn't finish her sentence.

My fingers are already at the button on her jeans. They're as soaked as her shirt, if not more so. The material clings to her as I yank it down, and she steps out of the wet denim.

Another garment on the floor.

She's gnawing on her bottom lip, and I lean forward, tasting her mouth, drinking her in. She tastes like honey and nectar, sweet and tantalizing.

Every nip and it doesn't feel like enough.

I'm starving for her.

Between fervent kisses, I pinch the band of her bra. The purple lacy satin falls down around her shoulders, and she holds her arm out of the shower to let it hit the floor.

Nikki doesn't stop me and I'm not one to hold back. If she doesn't want this, she'll tell me. She made that ultimately clear just a few nights ago.

I should make her beg.

Make her plead for my cock inside of her.

I nibble on her bottom lip and she leans into my body. Her hips are rocking. Is she aching for me the same way that I ache for her?

There's so much I want to say, but the words don't ever reach my lips. I rip the thin panties away and hear her tiny gasp as I tease her entrance with my cock.

She moans, and I continue teasing her.

My lips trail a path of warm kisses across her neck and down her collarbone.

Nikki tilts her head to the side, granting me access, offering herself to me.

I smile, pleased that she has fallen under my trance. My heart hammers in my chest as my tongue teases and sucks her breasts. I want to savor every second, prove to her that staying here is what she wants and not an obligation.

She can't leave.

I won't let her.

But I want her desire to stay to be stronger than my need for her to be here.

My head is cloudy, my thoughts slipping fast out of my reach. I drop down to the floor of the shower— the water pounds at my back.

I guide her legs farther apart and lick her slit. She shudders, and I've only just begun.

"Not yet, Kitten," I say. "You'll come when I give you permission."

She whimpers in protest. Her fingers tangle in my hair.

"Dante," she whispers my name. It's like heaven to my ears and makes my cock rock hard. I have to control myself if I want this to last, and I desperately do. I want her craving more from me when we're done, begging me for release.

"When was the last time you came?" I ask. My tongue laps at her folds and along her slit. Her wetness seeps out, a silent admission of her desire. I tease her clit, flicking it slowly with my tongue, barely grazing it at first.

She doesn't answer me.

"Was it with me?" I ask. My tongue grazes higher, circling her tiny pearl.

Her breathing quickens.

"Or did you touch yourself?" I stare up at her.

"Oh, God," she groans. The redness from the shower is nothing in comparison to the blush that stains her cheeks.

I guide one and then two fingers inside her warmth.

"Did you touch yourself since you've been here, under my roof?" I ask.

Her eyes slam shut, and she tightens onto my digits. "Look at me," I command.

When she doesn't obey, I withdraw my fingers and slowly pull my lips from her heated core.

She gasps and trembles, struggling to stand. I shut off the shower and lift her over my shoulder, carrying her into my bedroom.

"Dante?"

"You didn't answer my question," I say as I lay her on the bed on her stomach. I guide her bottom up into the air. "On all fours."

My fingers stroke her perfectly round bottom before teasing her folds apart. "Do you want me?" I lean forward, my breath teasing her ear.

"Yes," she whispers. Her answer is raspy and thick. Each breath Nikki takes is heavy, and her soft gasps turn quickly to moans as I position my cock at her entrance.

"Tell me you want me to fuck you." It takes every amount of self-restraint to keep from plunging into her. I'd usually grab a condom, but it seems a worthless investment now, seeing as how I've already knocked her up.

"Yes, I want you to fuck me," she purrs.

Her words are the most perfect sweet harmony that I've ever heard. I guide myself inside her tightness and reach around, teasing her clit with each thrust.

Nikki's head falls forward as her back arches. I can already feel her orgasm building as she trembles against my cock.

"Not yet," I warn and glide out of her.

She whimpers in protest, and I flip her around, tossing her onto her back. "You'd better not be done," she says, staring at my rock-hard cock.

I scoff under my breath.

Done?

Not until we're both screaming.

I plunge into her, harder and deeper. I guide her legs to my shoulders, and her insides tighten against me.

"Please." She's gnawing on her bottom lip again. Her eyes are open, but they are tiny slits as she struggles to stare up at me.

"You may come," I command as I rub her clit, and she's clenching and tightening. Her toes curl and her back arches off the mattress.

It takes every ounce of energy to hold on another few seconds as I listen to the soft gasps and moans as her orgasm overtakes her body.

One.

Two.

Three more strokes and I'm there with her, spilling myself inside of her, buried in her warmth.

I pull out and climb off the mattress, heading back to the bathroom.

"Dante?" Her voice is soft and sweet, like a faded whisper.

"Go to sleep," I say.

She climbs under the covers. My covers.

I never let anyone else sleep in my bed.

I stalk into the bathroom and shut the door.

What have I done?

Fucking her wasn't part of the equation.

She's the mother of my child. But a relationship? That could get complicated too fast. I lean on the bathroom counter. Staring at my reflection, I see my father, his hatred in my eyes.

I hate him.

I hate myself even more.

He was a cruel man, bringing countless women into his bed. It is any wonder that I'm his only child? I expected to discover a half-sibling somewhere out there, waiting to claim our father's inheritance.

It never happened.

I'm the unlucky bastard to have a father who didn't want a son. My mother died when I was young. I had countless nannies until I was of the age to attend boarding school.

I'll never send my own flesh and blood away, but raising a child, what the hell do I know about that?

There are monsters who roam the streets and want my family destroyed. How am I supposed to protect a baby?

I shut off the bathroom light and retreat to the bedroom. Nikki is already sound asleep and softly snoring, buried under my covers.

I can't stay in here with her.

Correction.

This is my room.

She can't stay in here with me.

I swing by my dresser, slip on a pair of boxers before I lift her with the blanket curled around her into my arms.

She stirs but doesn't fully wake. Her head lolls back to my chest. How is it that she's so peaceful and calm without a care in the world?

Nikki's tough. With all that she's endured because of her father, she's still living and breathing, smiling and oblivious to the monster that he is.

Well, I'm not quite sure I've seen her smile, but I am confident that she doesn't have the slightest clue that he had her abducted.

And I'm the asshole who doesn't get to tell her the truth.

Carrying her back into her room, I guide her under the covers and pull her blankets up around her. I refrain from giving her a kiss goodnight. She's not mine to tuck into bed. Not yet.

I retreat with my blankets and quietly close her bedroom door.

I've sworn a secret vow to keep the truth from her, to protect her.

20

NICOLE

I roll around beneath the covers and stretch my arm out to find the bed beside me empty.

Did he go to his office? Or back to work?

My eyes lazily flutter open. I'm back in my bedroom.

I exhale an exhaustive sigh and push myself out of bed. It's already morning, and the sun is bright.

It doesn't fit my mood. There should be thunderclouds rolling in and shaking the house.

The yellow of the sun casts the bedroom in a chipper glow.

I didn't shut the curtains last night before bed.

Apparently, Dante didn't think of it either before disposing of me back in my bedroom.

What the hell?

Was that all I was to him, a sex object? A quick fuck.

He did buy me from that stupid auction. I was a prisoner at his mercy. Grabbing the pillow, I throw it across the room.

It falls to the floor with barely a sound, not so much as a thud.

Why did I think I meant anything more to him?

He'd made it clear that I was his to own. He'd bought me like property after abducting me.

The bastard!

Was it all because of his stupid truck that I stole?

He knows my father is don. Isn't he scared Papa will do something to retaliate?

I still can't wrap my head around why Papa let Dante take me home.

Dante must not have given Papa a choice.

I have to give it time. Papa will send an army of men to obliterate Dante and his men.

But when?

Already, a week has passed and I'm still stuck here, unable to leave.

A sharp rap and the bedroom door swings open. It's one of the guards. "You are expected downstairs in five minutes," he says.

Expected? Now Dante is giving me orders?

"Or what?" I ask and pull the covers tight around myself. I'm naked beneath the bed sheets and don't want the guard to get any ideas. He barely looks old enough to drink. Although with friends like Dante, I'm sure he gets whatever he wants, liquor included.

"It's okay, Leone," Dante says to the guard. He steps past him and invites himself into my bedroom. Dante is fully dressed, expensive suit and all, with the shiny black shoes to finish his ensemble.

I try not to ogle him. But it's hard when that voice inside my head keeps nagging me.

He hurt you. He abducted you. Remember? Don't fall for his charm. Don't fall for him.

"We're having breakfast before I have to start my day."

Am I supposed to feel treasured that he's inviting me to eat breakfast with him? I don't give a crap. "I'm not hungry."

I roll over to protest his announcement. Maybe he'll get the hint and leave me alone. After all, he certainly did that last night after we—in his bed.

I grimace, just remembering the incident. I don't want to think about sex or think about him. And every second longer, the thought flitters through my head. I remember his hot, naked body.

No.

No.

No.

I mentally plug my ears and sing.

"You're not listening to a word I'm saying." Dante rips the blankets from my naked body.

"You bastard!" I screech and dive for the covers, which he has yanked off the bed. He's stronger and far more forceful than I am.

My fists pound at him, but he grabs my wrists and pins me back against the wall. My nipples harden from the chill in the air.

We're alone, just the two of us, and I'm naked. The door is wide open, and anyone could walk in. If Leone is nearby, he doesn't give any indication of his presence.

"I'm the bastard?" Dante laughs. "Funny, considering you're fighting me. I'm just defending myself."

"You're unreal." I can't believe him. Turning it around like I'm the bad guy. "You abducted me. Forced me to come home with you and locked me up in your precious castle. Do you honestly think you're the hero?"

The smile disappears from Dante's face. He drops his hold on me, takes a step back, and dusts off his jacket like I've just thrown fire at him.

His eyes flicker and narrow. There's something behind those dark depths that draws me in so easily.

I blame the hormones.

"I only invited you to join me for breakfast because you're carrying my child. It was a kindness I was extending. It won't happen again. A guard will bring you three meals a day," Dante says and turns on his heel.

He's unforgiving and fast. Dante storms out of the bedroom, slamming and locking the door behind himself.

I'm never getting out of here.

21

DANTE

"I want footage inside the DeLuca house," I say. I'm not satisfied with the audio equipment. I need more. Something that I can use on Gino to destroy him.

But how?

And what?

I sit at my desk, sinking into the midnight-black leather. I rake my fingers over the wood grains of the desk. I'm distracted.

Nikki has distracted me.

If I'm not careful, she could get me killed.

It's why I called a meeting with Moreno. I need his expertise and to bounce an idea off of him. I trust him above all others not only to have my back, but to tell me when I'm fucking up or wrong.

"Boss," Moreno says and clears his throat. He's been talking, but I haven't been listening.

I glance up at him. It's just the two of us.

"We can send in Halsey," Moreno says. "He knows the layout of the house, and he's already been inside once and got the job done. Besides, Breckenridge is small, the cable company doesn't have that many service techs. Gino will start noticing if every tech coming to his house is of Italian descent."

Shit.

He has a point.

"I'll think about it," I say.

I'm still waiting to hear from the Russians.

The DeLucas have their own private security system. If we can hack in and have remote access then I won't have to worry about risking my men.

It's an easy solution, but it will cost me a favor.

I rub the back of my neck. I'm tired. I didn't get enough sleep. Putting Nikki back in her bedroom, I had thought would help me sleep. It didn't. Instead, I smelled her scent all over my pillow and sheets.

I'll need to have the sheets changed and washed. Will that get her scent out of the room?

"Can we discuss Nicole?" Moreno asks.

He wouldn't bring her up unless there was something bothering him. He knows when to keep his mouth shut, which concerns me that he isn't doing so now.

"What is there to discuss? As you know, she's pregnant. I'm not just sending her off with my child, never to hear from again."

That isn't open for discussion.

If Moreno thinks keeping Nikki here is a bad idea, he will be in for a rude awakening. She isn't leaving until I set her free.

"She believes you're the bad guy."

"In case you missed the memo, I'm no saint."

Moreno rolls his eyes and leans back in the chair across from me. It tips back just slightly off the ground. "Yeah, well, my concern is that Gino has a plan that we haven't seen, and when he comes for Nicole, she'll be ready to go with him and give him all your secrets."

I've already thought that through. "Why do you think I keep her contained to her bedroom?" I don't let her anywhere near my locked office or my men. There is a guard who accompanies her to the kitchen, but that's the only place she's been allowed to roam except when she snuck out the other night.

That wasn't going to happen again.

"You can't do that forever," Moreno says.

I want to tell him try me, but I know he's right. "When the baby comes, there will be a nursery and her bedroom." I smirk in satisfaction.

"The girl needs vitamin D. Light. Sunshine. You know, the giant ball in the sky."

"I'm not an idiot," I say. "When she's less feisty, you can let her roam the garden. Keep a guard on her at all times. And I'm bulking up security around here. Once Gino gets wind that his daughter is pregnant, who knows what he will do."

"You said he gave you his blessing to marry his daughter. Was that not what happened?" Moreno asks.

"More or less." I wave dismissively. It strikes me as an odd bargain, but I don't want to overthink a man who would torment and torture his daughter. He's sick.

"About that nursery, boss. Do you want me to have a crib and essentials ordered and delivered to the premises?"

I know nothing about children. I'm surprised Moreno knows more than I do, but he does have two younger siblings. I'm an only child.

"Yes. A crib would be good. You take care of that. I'll deal with Nikki."

"Deal with her how?" Moreno asks. He raises an inquisitive eye, just one eyebrow lifts. I don't know how the hell he does that. Or if he's even trying.

"I'll remind her who is in charge. She has this way about her, Moreno. I swear she's trying to get under my skin. I need to break it out of her—that determination."

"She's not a puppy that you can train and take out to play with when you're bored."

"Isn't that precisely what she is? My pet."

Kitten.

22

NICOLE

He hadn't been lying when he told me a guard would bring me three meals a day. On most days, it is the young and possibly impressionable Leone.

He seems the most easily manipulated, but I haven't so much as tried to escape when he brings my food on a silver tray into my bedroom.

Where would I run?

Leone isn't the only guard.

When I've been escorted to the kitchen, I've counted as many as five men inside, easy to spot. There are more outside, and possibly others whom I haven't seen in the castle.

It has nearly been a week and not the slightest word or glance from Dante. I don't know if he is home and avoiding me or away on business.

What does he do other than abduct girls?

I perch myself at the edge of the windowsill. The platform is wide and plenty big. It could easily be a reading cubby if only my room had been filled with books. Someplace to take my mind.

I don't imagine that Dante reads much or anything at all. He doesn't seem the type to have his nose stuck in a book.

I miss the giant library back at home in Papa's house. There were always new books added for me to discover when I was bored.

"I've brought you dinner," Moreno says.

I glance up from my seat on the ledge of the window. If only I could actually open the damned pane. My fingernails trace the thick glue that's molded along with the windowpane.

"Don't waste your energy," Moreno says.

I drop my hand to my lap. He doesn't know what's running through my head.

"You brought—" My nose crinkles at the smell, and I run to the bathroom.

The morning sickness comes at every hour of the day, especially when food is brought to me.

"Venison," Moreno answers from the bedroom.

The tray clanks as he places it presumably on the table near the window.

After emptying the contents of my stomach, I flush, wash my hands, and slowly return to the bedroom.

"I'm not hungry," I say. In case it isn't already obvious.

"You've barely eaten today," Moreno says.

I give a mere shrug. Bringing a child into this world seems cruel. Am I not better off letting nature take its course?

The thought brings tears to my eyes, but I push it all down. I'm sure it's the stupid hormones causing my emotions to flare.

Dante hasn't even seen me in days. "Where is he?" I ask.

Moreno is more likely to tell me the truth. I've gotten nothing out of Leone. However, I don't know if he has no answer or just won't tell me anything.

"You should eat," Moreno says, "or I will have to tell him."

Good.

"That's what it takes to get his attention?" I scoff under my breath and fold my arms across my chest.

I'm tired of the games. I'm a prisoner, and while the accommodations are nicer than the compound, it's still me without my freedom.

I need to escape, to feel the warm summer breeze on my skin. Glancing out at the sun through the window doesn't offer the same appeal.

Moreno stares at me. His eyes crinkle slightly. "Is there something else I can get for you? Any cravings?"

Dante's second seems to care more about my well-being than the father of my child.

"Bring me Dante."

He exhales a heavy sigh. "I'll leave you with your food," Moreno says, ignoring my request. He retreats from the bedroom, and I hear the door click and the lock snap into place.

———

After telling Moreno to bring me Dante, I'm not sure what I expect to happen. I perch myself on the ledge of the window, staring out into the backyard, the open expanse that stretches on as far as I can see.

I grab the butter knife from the tray and work the glue loose around the window. Maybe I can manage an escape.

I'm hard at work, chipping away at the sticky residue that clings to the window when Dante bolts into the room.

When Moreno enters without knocking, it's calm and tranquil. Not Dante. He blows in like a storm.

My fingers drop the knife, and it clanks loudly as it tumbles to the floor while I shift quickly to hide what I've been doing. I suspect he already knows.

Is that why he chose now to come?

Are there cameras in my bedroom?

Or was it my request to Moreno for Dante to visit that brought him thundering into my room?

My mouth is dry, parched. There's a glass of water with my meal that sits untouched.

"Is it necessary that I feed you?" Dante asks. His face shows no hint of emotion, but it doesn't match his exterior. His hands are bunched into fists at his sides.

Does he not want to come speak to me? Is it Moreno who forced his hand? That seems unlikely.

Dante doesn't do anything that he doesn't want. A benefit of being the boss.

"I'm not hungry," I say and glance at the plate of food that's now no doubt grown cold.

He steps farther into the room, closer toward me. He doesn't comment about the knife that clanked to the floor. Instead, he bends down and picks it up, keeping it from me.

"What will you eat?" he asks.

"I told you. I'm not hungry." Consider it a hunger strike. Well, that and morning sickness. The thought of food makes me queasy.

"No sweet tooth? Or maybe you crave a salty snack? Can I bring you a bag of potato chips? I'll bring you anything you want."

The nerve of him! "Do you really think a bag of chips makes up for the fact you've locked me in your house and stolen my freedom?"

"It's not safe for you out there." He points toward the window. "Do you know what I went through to bring you back here with me?"

I don't like him being this close within my personal space. I need room to breathe. I skirt off the ledge.

My feet are filled with nervous energy. Sitting isn't an option.

"It couldn't have been that difficult," I say. "Your men forced me into their car and abducted me!" How dare he play the victim, like he isn't the one entirely in control.

My stomach roils and I'm sure any moment I'm going to be sick again.

"I want you out of here!" I point to the door. "Go!" I shout, but he doesn't listen.

Bile rises to my mouth, and I rush to the bathroom, flipping the lid of the toilet.

I should have just left it up. I spend more time with my head bent over the porcelain bowl than anything else in that room.

I startle when he rests a hand on my back.

I'm sweaty and gross.

I flush and wash my hands. "You want to do something for me?"

He stares at me.

"Get me mouthwash."

23

DANTE

I don't like the reports that I hear from Leone and Moreno that Nikki has barely touched her food.

Moreno had mentioned that she's suffering from apparent morning sickness, and that's probably why she hasn't eaten.

Is it pure defiance?

No.

When she rushes into the bathroom, there is no faking her bringing up bile.

And somehow, she finds it in her to joke about getting her mouthwash.

I bend down and open the cupboard under the sink. I hand her a brand-new bottle of mint-flavored mouthwash.

She purses her lips and scrunches up her face. Apparently, she's not as much of a snoop as I'd have thought.

Then again, it was in the bathroom that was for her to use. Maybe I should start listening to Moreno and let her out of her bedroom, give her a little more leeway.

But can I trust her?

She peels open the plastic and pours a small amount into a dixie cup, swooshing and spitting into the sink.

"Anything else? Soup? Crackers? Hot tea?" I suggest.

Things haven't been great between us. I'm as much to blame as she is, but that's beside the point. I'm honestly worried about her. I'm also concerned about the baby that she's carrying, my child.

"As I said, I'm not hungry." She brushes past me and slumps onto the mattress. It's like the fire inside of her is blown out. Defeated.

I'm not used to seeing her like this.

I thought her lack of hunger was more out of a strike than anything else, but looking at her, examining her more closely, I'm concerned.

She's lost a lot of weight. Shouldn't she be putting on weight by now?

"I'm taking you to the hospital. Stay right there," I say and step out into the hallway to find Moreno. I let him know that I'm concerned about Nikki's well-being and to keep an eye on things while we're gone.

He'll have it handled.

Moreno brings my truck around to the front, freshly washed and detailed after its return. It's been parked around the side, untouched.

I gather Nikki into my arms and carry her down the stairs and out the front door.

She squints under the evening sun that's bright but not blinding. I should take Moreno's advice and let her outside, but it's hard for me to trust her. How can I when she's Gino's daughter?

At any moment, she could betray me.

How do I know that she's not a plant to get intelligence for the DeLuca family?

It has certainly crossed my mind. Why else would he allow me the opportunity to marry his daughter? Just because he doesn't want her to know he was behind her abduction seems far-fetched, even for Gino.

My stomach twists at the mere idea that Nikki is playing with me to gain freedom of my home. The office is locked, and the secrets that could destroy me aren't kept out in the open for her to stumble upon.

I'm not careless.

Everything I do is calculated.

"I don't want to go to the hospital," she mumbles against my chest. But she doesn't fight me.

I place her gently on the passenger seat of the truck and she groans.

Does it bring back memories of her stealing my vehicle? I hope she enjoyed her stubborn and reckless streak because, as far as I'm concerned, it's over.

"I know, but I'm worried about you. You can't keep anything down." At the very least, she should have an ultrasound. I'd been neglecting my duties, and while I appreciated our physician coming to see her on such short notice the night she arrived at my home, he's not an obstetrician.

I want only the best doctor to care for my child.

And for Nikki.

————

It's not a quick drive to the nearest hospital across the mountain. Life flights where we live are incredibly common because there aren't really any ambulances.

For most injuries and illnesses, we have a local physician, Dr. Reiss, who works closely with the family, but he's an older gentleman, and I'm not sure what he knows about delivering babies. He's good with a needle and thread, patching up bullet holes, and emergency surgeries.

We don't have too many women around the castle and even less who are pregnant.

Nikki is the first.

I'm determined to get Nikki an ultrasound to ensure the health of our little prize growing inside her. I need to know that our baby is doing all right.

Whether she wants me to accompany her or not in the emergency room, I'm at her side like the doting father one might expect.

On this side of the mountain, I'm not a familiar face. I don't frequent the hospital if I don't have to. In fact, I avoid it at all costs.

Nikki has no idea of the risks I've taken to bring her here. My enemies extend far beyond the borders of Breckenridge, and I'm without guards and men backing me up.

I should have brought one of the soldiers to have my back, but it's too late now. My focus needs to be on her.

She's lying on a hospital bed, a small white cot, with a blanket draped over her. The nurse is filling out paperwork, jotting down information while Nikki is forthcoming with answers to the questions that the nurse asks.

I've never seen Nikki quite so calm or kind.

Is that how she'll be with our baby?

Or have I worn the fight out of her?

Doubtful.

Time always seems to stand still in the emergency room every time I've been behind these stark white double doors. Usually, I'm covered in blood, the weight of another's life on my hands.

This time it's not my men in danger.

I squeeze Nikki's hand. Her eyes are glassy, her lips dry.

A nurse brings her a cup of ice chips, and she obliges, sucking on them one at a time. She hasn't said much, and I never leave her side.

Am I worried that she'll tell the hospital staff that I've taken her against her will?

The thought flickers across my mind. I don't let it stick.

The technician brings over the ultrasound equipment.

"We're going to listen to your baby's heartbeat and take some pictures." Before Nikki can answer one question, the technician asks another one.

"Have you two done this before? Are you ready?" the young woman asks. She's all smiles and a bit too bubbly for my taste.

Nikki must think the same thing, because she glances at me with desperate eyes. Does she want me to shut the woman up?

The only way I know how isn't appropriate at a hospital.

Nikki lifts her shirt, and the flatness of her stomach strikes me. Should she be showing? I know it's only been a few weeks, but there's not even the slightest hint of a belly.

The technician applies a generous amount of clear goopy jelly over Nikki's stomach before pressing the wand down and examining the monitor.

I see the littlest speckle on the monitor. It's hardly bigger than a grape—the thumping of a pulse jets through the speaker.

Our baby's heartbeat.

I press my lips tight together.

The air is sucked out of my lungs. The room spins.

I'm going to be a father.

"Wow," Nikki says. She squeezes my hand, her grip undeniable and tight. Fear crosses over her brow.

Is she afraid of me or what this baby means? Her life will never be the same, and neither will mine.

I can't keep treating her like a prisoner.

Moreno is right. I have to grant her sunlight and freedom, even if it's just a taste.

But she has no idea how much she's in danger, all because of me.

24

NICOLE

The drive home is met with silence. I stare out the window of the truck.

Dante hasn't said more than two words to me since we left.

That was over an hour ago.

I can't tell if he's mad or just lost in his thoughts. I rest my eyes and doze off until we arrive back at the castle.

It's dark outside, and for the first time in days, my stomach isn't churning. The doctor prescribed some medication and gave me an I.V. while at the hospital. That probably helped for the time being.

Dante parks the truck out front and rushes around when I open the door.

"Here, let me help you."

His men are already at the door. Moreno opens the front entrance, and Leone is right beside him. Behind him are two other men who I've seen around the premises from time to time, but I don't know their names.

Something's happened. I can feel the heaviness in the air.

Dante must sense it, too.

"What is it?" he asks.

Moreno glances at me. He's hesitating. Is my father coming to rescue me from this prison?

Why has it taken so long? I truly believed he would have come sooner.

I rest a hand over my abdomen and make my way up the stairs. I know the route up to my bedroom. I don't need an escort.

Yet, I feel him on my heels.

Dante is following me.

"Planning on locking me in my room?" I quip over my shoulder. I'm tired of the games.

I will escape. It's only a matter of time.

"I don't believe that is necessary," he says.

I stop outside my bedroom door and spin around to face him. His breath is warm, and there's an obvious charge in the air.

"Why is that?" I should be grateful he's not going to lock me in my room, but I'm surprised. I want to know why the sudden change in his demeanor.

"You won't leave."

What makes him confident that I won't run and betray him the first chance that I get?

"You won't let me leave," I counter. If I had the freedom to go, I would.

He turns the handle to my bedroom and opens the door. Dante gestures for me to step inside. He flips on the overhead light and then walks toward the bedside table, turning the small lamp on as well.

With a sigh, I trail into the bedroom. I doubt he will stay. He never stays. He usually comes in, chews off my head, we fight, and then he leaves.

That's the only pattern that we've established. Why would tonight be any different?

"How are you feeling?" Dante asks. His eyes flicker. I don't know what he's thinking. Feeling.

"The medicine helped." I point to the door. "I left my prescription in your truck." Technically, he left the prescription and paperwork in the truck. Dante had taken it from the doctor. He hadn't let me handle anything on my own.

"I will have one of my men pick up your prescription," Dante says. "In the meantime, you should get some rest. Unless you're hungry? I could have the chef whip you up something to eat."

While I'm no longer nauseous, I am tired. "Sleep sounds good." I patter toward the dresser and pull out a tank top and shorts to wear to bed. Eventually, I will need another wardrobe. "Dante?"

"Yes."

"I'm going to need new clothes, again. Pretty soon, I'm going to start showing." I'm hoping he will let me accompany him out to the stores, the market, anywhere outside the castle that I've been locked inside.

"And when you do, I will make certain Moreno picks up enough clothes to fit you."

I exhale a heavy breath. "That isn't what I meant." He knows what I meant. He has to. Dante isn't an idiot. I'd suspect that he's avoiding letting me leave. Is he afraid that I won't come back?

He should be afraid.

"We will talk about it another day," Dante says and clears his throat. "Right now, you're in no condition to be wandering stores. You need to be getting the nausea under control and eating more calories. If you don't like what our chef prepares, I can kill him and have someone else brought in to cook for you."

"No!" I gasp. My mouth drops, and I recognize that smile on his face. "You bastard!" I smack his arm. I can't believe his antics.

He quirks a grin. "I had you."

"You'll never have me, Dante," I say.

His lips are a firm line, and his brow creases as he considers my words.

He can't have me because I'm not his to have. Not so long as I'm forced to live in his castle, under his command, with no ounce of freedom.

He can own my body but not my heart.

Dante slips past me. His hands rest on my hips as he guides me to sit on the edge of the mattress. "Never is a long time," he whispers.

His breath is warm and delectable. It sends a shiver through my insides. I try to hide the shudder, but he smiles knowingly. He's proud that he can arouse me with such a simple touch.

I hate him for it. I hate how my body betrays me. I want to hate Dante. It would be easier to scream at him and tell him that he's a monster. But the truth is I can't do that. I'm bound to him in a way that goes deeper than even I care to admit. It's not just the baby that attaches me to him.

There's more to it.

The longing for something that I've never had, never experienced before.

I can't explain it. I'm not sure that I want to, either. It makes me uncomfortable, like an itchy sweater that I want to peel off and burn.

"You could have destroyed me today." He brushes a strand of hair behind my ear and then dips my chin back to meet his stare.

His eyes are fueled with want and need. Hunger. Desire. Arousal.

I swallow the lump in my throat.

"How?" I don't feel like I have any amount of power, even minute.

"At the hospital," Dante says. "You could have come up with any number of reasons to not let me in the room with you."

He leans closer, his forehead coming to rest against mine, and I emit a soft moan from the back of my throat.

I hate him for dragging me to his home, keeping me here, but he hasn't been unkind. I've been treated better under his direct care than I had those handful of days at the compound.

There hadn't been the right time to tell a nurse that I'd been held against my will.

Dante was always at my side. Doting. Loving. Affectionate. He isn't that man back in Breckenridge.

The hospital staff doesn't know him the same way that I do. To them, he is just a concerned father. To me, he is my abductor, my captor, and the father of my unborn baby.

Two of those things I couldn't help. The third, I would ensure no matter what that he never saw through.

If he is beginning to trust me, then I will use that to my advantage.

Dante will never come near my child.

25

DANTE

I tuck Nikki into bed beneath the covers and shut the door. I don't lock her in. Not tonight.

Stepping out into the hallway, Moreno is waiting for me.

"How bad is it?" Moreno asks.

"The baby is fine. I should be asking you that question." I try to keep my voice down and gesture that we take this someplace else.

We head for my office downstairs. I brush past Leone. "Keep post outside Nicole's door," I instruct. While she may not be locked in her bedroom, I need to know what she's doing. "Eyes on her at all times if she's not in her room."

"Yes, boss." Leone tromps up the stairwell.

Moreno and I head into my office. I unlock the door and flick on the light, shutting the door behind us.

"Anything?" The fact all the capos are at my home in the middle of the night tells me something is brewing, and Moreno has news for me.

"We got eyes and ears inside the DeLuca mansion," Moreno says. "Your visit with the Russians paid off."

I should be relieved, but the stone in the bottom of my stomach sinks like a submarine.

"What's the cost?" I ask. They must have reached out to Moreno when they couldn't get ahold of me at the hospital.

"They want involvement in our arms deal. Ten percent as a silent partner."

"Fuck!" I'd have negotiated it down but Moreno had the authority to act as don while I was unreachable.

Moreno's face is grim. "That's not why the capos are here, boss."

Exhaling a heavy breath, I feel the weight of trouble coming down on my shoulders. "How bad is it?"

Moreno powers up the tablet and opens a specific file. "This was recorded around midnight."

He hands me the device, and I stare at the men on the screen. I recognize them. Gino is on the right. He's speaking with Vance and Rafael. Vance is his right-hand man, the same as Moreno is to me.

The last time I saw Rafael and Gino was at the soiree. I'm not sure what I'm expecting to see, to hear, to pay witness to as I slump into my desk chair.

The tablet stays latched in my grip.

"Are you ever going to tell me your end game with Nicole? No way you'd let that vermin marry your daughter for money," Rafael asks.

"I've been wondering the same thing, boss," Vance says.

"That spoiled brat was just like her mother. Needs a lesson or two in humility if you ask me. Abducting her was brilliant, and even better, she thinks Dante was her captor." A wide grin spreads across his face. His eyes crinkle. "It's never been about my end game. It's about my motivation. My deception. My desire to destroy."

"Destroy. How?" Vance asks.

"Tick-tock," Gino says cryptically.

I pause the video. "What am I missing?" There were hours of recordings and footage already to filter through. I didn't have the time or energy to sift through it. That's what my men were supposed to do.

"Keep watching," Moreno says.

I'm not sure that I can. Every time I look at Gino, I want to throw the damned video across the room.

Exhaling a heavy sigh, I hit resume.

"Tick-tock," Gino repeats.

"The mouse ran up the clock?" Rafael shakes his head. "I don't get it, boss."

Neither did I. What was I missing? I listened to the message. I waited to understand what it meant.

"Nicole has been poisoned," Gino says.

Vance's brow furrows, and he stands to pace the room. "Why? You couldn't possibly have known Dante was going to show up and suggest buying your daughter."

"Of course not. We drug the girls, so they're less likely to fight. Nicole took a heavier dose, and when she was out with the last batch, we mixed in a special cocktail. She's been a problem lately. One who needs discipline. I thought after she'd be sick and on her deathbed that she'd come to see I was doing right by her."

"But now she's with the Riccis," Rafael says. "Are we going to abduct her? Bring her home?"

"No. We'll send flowers and our condolences. She's already exhibiting symptoms, I'm sure of it. She'll be dead in forty-eight hours."

I drop the device at the desk. "Nikki's dying?"

26

NICOLE

The bedroom squeaks open, stirring me from slumber. I roll over on the mattress, my eyes sore and dry. I'm tired. Who is coming into my room?

Shadows dance over his darkened features.

I'd recognize that body anywhere. What is he doing sneaking into my bedroom?

"Dante?" I rub the sleep from my eyes. "What are you doing?" I sit up in bed and pull the covers up tight around myself.

He's quiet and stalking me like I'm his prey. Dante climbs atop the bed, hovering over me, forcing me to lie back down.

"You—"

"What?" I ask. The glint of sadness in his eyes makes my stomach churn.

The hospital had affirmed that the baby was healthy with an ultrasound.

There's something behind those dark eyes that has my heart aching, wanting to know what's wrong.

He leans down and his lips capture mine in a searing hot kiss. With one hand, his fingers tangle in my hair, pulling me closer, tighter as he lowers himself against me, trapping me between him and the bed.

"Tell me what it is," I whisper between kisses.

My body instantly responds to his touch, his warmth and his desire poking at me. A moan slips past my lips, and he takes it as further encouragement, pushing the sheets down, his hips lifting long enough to climb under the covers with me.

"I want you," Dante says.

Straddling my hips, he shucks his shirt and removes my t-shirt. I lift my hips to allow him to slide my pajama bottoms and panties down. It's hard to deny him anything when his kisses ignite a fire inside me.

It's probably the hormones raging through my body making me crave his touch.

His breath teases a path down my neck, and he nips at my skin, marking me.

I am his.

He wants everyone to know that I belong to him.

Isn't that why I'm locked in this castle?

"Roll over," he demands into my ear, and he swiftly flips me over, his hands strong against my hips. "On all fours."

Even in sex, he commands with authority. A shiver courses down my spine as I crawl onto my knees.

He guides my legs farther apart, and his touch between my thighs sends a ripple of heat surging to my core.

"You're wet for me. Good, Kitten," he whispers into my ear.

"Yes, Master," I say, playing the part that he must so deliberately want of me. Why else give me a pet name and command me at his will to do as he demands?

He rewards me. Dante's fingers glide between my folds and then circle my clit.

I rock my hips back and forth, his fingers putting the perfect amount of pressure on my aching bead.

"I know you want to come," Dante whispers into my ear.

I whimper in agreement. He is right. I do want to experience that sweet release that he can offer me. Will he continue to tease me or grant me what I desire?

"Please," I rasp. I'm not above begging. That will come next as the desire fuels inside of me. I want to feel him fill me.

I reach around behind me, but he swats my hands away and nips my neck. His body is nestled up against mine, and his thick, hard cock pokes at my entrance.

"Do you want me to fuck you, Kitten?" Dante whispers into my ear.

"Yes."

My insides throb, and he hasn't even touched my warm, wet center. He's teased me, his fingers grazing my slit, but my insides crave more.

The pulsating sensation begins, and my toes curl. I want to feel his cock inside of me.

Dante teases the head of his cock against my entrance, and my hips buck, wanting him to enter me, to fuck me. I'm growing mad with want. The desire is turning to need.

"Please," I beg, and I feel his cock bury into my tightness.

A groan spills out past my lips, and my fingers clench at the bunched-up sheets tangled on the bed. My head is bent forward, hanging down, my back arched.

Every thrust, and I'm seeing stars. My eyes slam shut.

I give up trying to keep quiet. I know we're not alone in the castle, and yet I no longer care who can hear us.

My moans are much more pronounced and vocalized, which only seem to encourage Dante further.

Each thrust grows in intensity, his movements quickening the pace as he hears my moans. "Nikki," he grunts, and my insides clench down, pulsating around him.

Several more strokes, and I'm trembling in his grasp, toes curling. I don't wait for him, the sweet release making my heart pound against my ribcage like it might burst out of my chest.

Dante is right there with me, spilling himself inside of me before he rolls us around and collapses on the mattress, tugging me to lie above him.

I never thought he'd want to cuddle. He pulls me close, his fingers stroke my back and over my naked bottom.

Sweat covers my skin, and the cool air from the ceiling fan caresses me along with his touch.

I want to ask him what's going on, but his touch is soothing, and I'm drawn toward sleep. For the first time in days, I feel relieved, tranquil, and at peace.

"Goodnight," I mumble before drifting to sleep.

27

DANTE

How can I tell her the truth? Her hand is splayed over my chest, her breathing slow and even.

She's fallen asleep.

I pull the covers up around our naked bodies. I hadn't intended to come into her room to have sex with her, but seeing her, knowing that her father poisoned her, I can't ignore the feelings that stir inside of me.

I shouldn't feel something for Nikki. It's dangerous. Loving someone will destroy everything that I've achieved.

And yet that ultrasound this evening stole my heart.

She's having my child.

I can't ignore the growing feeling in the pit of my stomach, the sensation that when she's near, I'm distracted. I don't want to be lost in thoughts of a woman who should be my enemy.

Nikki is nothing like her father. At least as far as I can tell.

She's smart and cunning but not ruthless.

It's a relief to feel her soft breath against my chest as she sleeps. She's alive. My baby is alive. But for how much longer? What Gino said about her having forty-eight hours to live. How can that be?

I want to punch someone and scream.

Nikki shifts slightly, and my grip on her tightens. I never want to let her go.

Ever.

Could Gino be wrong? Maybe he suspects we're listening and is feeding us bad information? We only have audio surveillance in Gino's office. He couldn't have found the bug.

Do I take Nikki back to the hospital? Going there once was risky. Twice is deadly. If not for her, then for me.

There are men who want me dead. Showing up in the next town over is suicide. I have to tread carefully.

"Dante?"

"I'm right here," I whisper and rub her back soothingly. I want to lull her back to sleep. Could I be so lucky?

She tries to pull away and roll onto her side, but I don't let her go. My grip tightens around her waist.

"My arm is asleep," she says and tries to shift against me.

Reluctantly, I loosen my grip, and she shifts off my body and rolls onto her back. Her fingers graze my hip, her touch soft and lingering even as her fingers glide across my stomach and wander lower.

I trap her hand against my skin.

"If you keep that up—"

"You'll what?" she interrupts me. A huge smile spreads across her face.

Is she taunting me?

"What will the big ole' don do?" Nikki asks.

Yes, she's asking for it.

Why am I surprised?

Growling, I pin her down and trap her against the mattress, her arms held above her head by one of my hands. My other hand skims her hips as she writhes beneath me.

Her movements make my cock harden.

She's a temptress, and I cannot deny her pleasure.

Any thought of sleep is gone for both of us as I bury myself deep inside her warmth. Her legs wrap around me, pulling me tighter.

I capture her lips.

I need her.

Want her.

She's my own brand of drug, and my lips crash hard on hers, my tongue pushing inside her mouth.

Her moans are soft. Her hips match my thrusts, her back arching off the mattress. Her body is clawing at me without the use of her hands, pulling me tighter, desperate for release.

"Dante," she rasps my name between heated kisses, and her insides clamp down, trembling and pulsating.

It's enough to drive me over the edge with her.

Fuck.

Gasping for breath, I collapse onto the bed and roll off her body. I don't want to crush her or the baby growing inside of her.

Losing her isn't an option. Not now. Not ever.

28

NICOLE

"You're still here," I whisper. Dante is curled up beside me.

I didn't expect that he'd last the entire night in my bed. Something has come over him. I'm just not sure what it is.

It's no surprise he's keeping secrets, but there's something that he isn't telling me that has me worried.

"I am." He presses his lips tight together. "How are you feeling?"

A faint smile curls at the top of my lips. "The nausea seems to be gone."

I don't know how long it will last, and I don't care. Right now, I'm just grateful not to be hanging my head over the toilet this morning.

"That's good."

He doesn't look thrilled with my news.

"What is it?" I don't have to know him that well to see that he's got a lot on his mind, what I can't determine if it's his job, the family, or me complicating matters.

"We should get dressed, breakfast, and then I'd like you to come into my office for a few minutes this morning. I'd like to show you something."

I don't have the slight notion of what he intends to show me, but the thought of escaping the confines of my room and exploring the castle a little more sounds pleasant enough.

"Sure," I say. I pull the sheets around myself and climb off the mattress.

It's the first real smile I've seen Dante quirk, and he's got the most adorable dimple on his right cheek.

Finding a t-shirt and black yoga pants, I grab that with a pair of panties and head for the bathroom.

There's not a door. Not even a semblance of privacy, thanks to Dante and his crew. "Do you mind?" I ask, gesturing for him to turn around or at least pretend not to stare into the bathroom.

"Yeah, it's my house." He folds his arms across his chest and doesn't even attempt to glance away.

"Well, this is my bedroom. In case you've forgotten, you've locked me up in here." I point at the door. "It's time for you to leave. And don't you dare take my sheets with you."

Dante stands.

Is he listening to me? That would be a first.

"I should get dressed." He bends down, grabs his boxers off the floor, and slips them on before leaving the bedroom.

I grumble under my breath and drop the bedsheet.

Sometimes he can be such an ass.

I dress and comb my hair before heading out of my bedroom. I turn the handle and poke my head out.

Dante is waiting for me.

"Where are the guards?" I ask.

There's no way that he left my door unlocked and didn't have a security detail, making sure that I didn't attempt to escape.

Though, let's face it, how far could I get? There are guards outside the property and plenty more inside. And with his security system to boot, I'm not going anywhere without help.

"Busy." Dante is cryptic as always.

He accompanies me down to the kitchen, and I grab a seat while he opens the fridge and retrieves a few breakfast staples: milk, orange juice, and creamer for coffee.

He pours one cup of coffee.

I clear my throat. "Do you have another cup?" I'll get it myself if he doesn't oblige.

Dante glances over his shoulder at me. "You're pregnant."

"I'm not dead," I remark and slip out of the chair and stand beside him at the cabinet. I flip the cabinet door open and grab a mug from the shelf. "Pour me a cup." It's not a question.

"Demanding, aren't we?" Dante smiles, but his eyes aren't full of mirth. There's a glimpse of darkness, but I have yet to unravel what is going on inside his head.

Will I ever?

Dante pours coffee into my mug, and I carry the hot drink back to the table to sit.

"You do know caffeine isn't healthy for a pregnant woman?"

"Neither is being held captive, and that hasn't stopped you from keeping me a prisoner under your roof." I ignore his dark gaze and reach for the cream and sugar, fixing my coffee the way I like to drink it. Sweet and not the least bit bitter.

Dante puts a dollop of cream but no sugar. It still looks black to me.

He has yet to answer my remark about being his prisoner.

What's there to say? It's true, and he knows it.

————

Breakfast is awkward at best. I don't think we've spent nearly as much time together as we have since last night.

Maybe it's not breakfast that's awkward, but the fact we had sex twice last night.

I hold no regrets, but does he? Then again, why else did he buy me and bring me home? That was what he bought me for, wasn't it? I chew my bottom lip raw as he leads me to his office.

I'm not sure what to expect or why he's leading me to his private locked suite. Is he expecting another round to satisfy his needs?

"What are we doing?" I ask as he unlocks the frosted glass door to his office. It's impossible to see anything until he opens the door and gestures me inside.

"I want you to see something."

Damn, is he cryptic? I purse my lips and step inside. I'm already his prisoner. If I don't follow his orders, he'll probably pick my ass up and carry me inside his office.

The thought is tempting, but I don't feel like being man-handled.

Inside his office is a dark mahogany desk and a black leather chair. Across is a seat for a guest, but it looks hardly worn. He probably doesn't get many visitors.

The walls are a dull gray, painted over wooden boards that brighten the room, which has no windows. There's a door inside his office, wood, and the handle has another lock.

I can't help but wonder what secrets he hides behind that door.

Dante steps around behind his desk and unlocks the desk drawer, gliding the wood drawer open. He retrieves a tablet. He taps the screen, unlocking it and opening up whatever app he apparently wants me to see.

What could he possibly want to show me?

"You should sit down," Dante says as he gestures to the guest chair across from his desk.

While I'd rather stand, the darkness in his gaze reappears, and I sink into the chair wordlessly.

He hits play and hands me the tablet to watch a video of my papa, Rafael, and Vance in Papa's office. "You're spying on my family?"

My stomach sinks, and the food I've eaten is somersaulting in my stomach.

"You need to watch the video," Dante says. He's calm. Too calm, given the sadness that passes across his gaze.

I shouldn't be surprised, and yet I'm disgusted that there is no privacy. "Did you plant cameras in this house, too? What about my bedroom?"

I shove my hands onto my lap to keep them steady, but I'm trembling both inside and out. This knowledge has me riled up inside.

Why did I think that I could trust him?

He doesn't answer my question, and I stand and drop the tablet at his desk.

"Sit!" Dante cracks like lightning, and his voice bellows and echoes off of the walls like thunder.

I drop back into my seat.

Dante presses play and forces me to watch the video.

"Nicole has been poisoned," Papa says.

Vance stands, his hands bunched into fists as he paces the room. "Why? You couldn't possibly have known Dante was going to show up and suggest buying your daughter."

"Of course not. We drug the girls, so they're less likely to fight. Nicole took a heavier dose, and when she was out with the last batch, we mixed in a special cocktail. She's been a problem lately. One who needs discipline. I thought after she'd be sick and on her deathbed that she'd come to see I was doing right by her."

"But now she's with the Riccis," Rafael says. "Are we going to abduct her? Bring her home?"

"No. We'll send flowers and our condolences. She's already exhibiting symptoms, I'm sure of it. She'll be dead in forty-eight hours."

"No. It's not—that's not my papa." The room is hot and suffocating under Dante's scrutiny. I escape from the chair and bolt out of his office.

I tear down the hall. The room spins, and I grip the wall to hold myself upright.

It doesn't work.

Dante is two steps behind, and as I sink to the ground, he catches me, scooping me up into his arms.

"He would never," I begin, but I can't finish my thoughts. It doesn't make sense.

Did Papa drug me?

No.

He isn't a monster. Dante is the monster. It has to be a trick—some type of video manipulation.

"Let me go." Even if Dante releases his hold on me, I don't think I can stand. The room is spinning wildly, and my stomach is doing somersaults. I'm not sure that I won't pass out or vomit. Either seems a plausible reality.

Dante wordlessly carries me up the flight of stairs to my bedroom.

I hate how even I've designated it my bedroom. It isn't mine. It shouldn't be mine. I don't want to stay.

He lays me down above the sheets. The bed is made. Dante has servants who tend to his every need. Were they bought in the same way that I was purchased and brought to his home?

"I hate you," I say. I feel the softness of the bed beneath my body. It's a welcoming distraction from my jelly legs, but I don't want to be in here. I don't want to be his. I should never have slept with him at the bar.

Is that what started this catastrophe? Or had it been that I stole his stupid truck?

He perches himself at the edge of my bed. He hasn't said a word to me. His silent treatment is worse than anything else. Why won't he argue and fight back?

Even uninvited on the bed, he seems relaxed, like he belongs.

Well, he doesn't.

"It's a trick. A lie. I don't believe you."

"Your father is a monster." Dante brushes a strand of hair out of my eyes.

I raise my hand to smack his arm away.

He grabs my wrist and holds it firmly. Is he reminding me that he's in charge? How could I ever forget?

His eyes flicker. And it's the same darkness, the sadness and brooding that I saw last night and again this morning.

"The video is real." Dante stares down at me.

When I stop fighting, he releases his tight grip on my wrist. My arm falls to my side.

"We are bringing in a physician to examine you this morning."

"I feel fine." My stomach is filled with dread, but I suspect it's more the news than anything else. "I went to the hospital last night. The ultrasound showed everything was fine. Our baby is healthy." I rest a hand over my abdomen.

"You've been losing weight, struggling to eat for the last couple of weeks. Moreno has a buddy who is a specialist in this kind of thing."

I roll my eyes. "I'm pregnant. It's not unusual to suffer from morning sickness." I shift to sit and prove to him that I'm fine and he is overreacting. But the room spins.

It is probably stress-related. He sure as hell is stressing the crap out of me.

"Fine. I'll let your specialist examine me, but I'm telling you I'm fine. My father wouldn't poison me."

Would he?

I rub my eyes. They sting, but I don't want him to see me react.

"Can I have some space?" I gesture for the door.

"I'll be just outside your room if you need anything."

I scoff under my breath. "I'm sure you will."

Dante stands and heads out of the room, leaving the door wide open.

Did he just give me permission to leave my room? He did say that he wasn't locking me in anymore. While I don't believe him, this is a first.

Maybe he just wants to watch and make sure I don't keel over and die.

There's a shuffle of footsteps, and Dante is speaking with someone out in the hallway. With the door wide open, they're talking quieter than usual. There are no muffled voices behind a door. If they speak a little louder, I can hear everything.

Dante steps out of sight, but he's still in the hallway.

I slide my legs over the edge of the mattress and stand on wobbly legs—one foot in front of the other.

My stomach is sour, but I chalk it up to the video and news. The baby is fine. I'm fine. Dante is a hypochondriac at best. At worst, he's trying to manipulate me.

Papa wouldn't hurt me. I'm sure of it.

It's a trick—a form of manipulation. Maybe Dante's men are behind it.

Dante wants me to stay because I'm having his child. But his men, they'd just as soon I leave. I'm sure I'm a distraction from the business.

I'll play along. I'll let his silly doctor examine me. Maybe if I pretend to be sick, the men who guard me will let their defenses down, and I can escape.

29

DANTE

After the doctor's thorough examination of Nikki, we step out into the hallway. I shut the door.

"What's the diagnosis?" I ask.

The doctor is an older gentleman and could easily be my father's age. His salt and pepper hair is short and wiry, flailing in every direction. He has the features of a mad scientist with his white lab coat and a stethoscope around his neck.

But I trust him.

He comes highly recommended.

"Aside from the pregnancy? She's been poisoned and has Ace Fever. I'd go so far as to say that it was used as a biological weapon given your situation. Whoever did this intended for Nikki to suffer. It's good you reached out when you did."

I swallow the lump in my throat. "And what about the baby?"

"She's at risk for miscarriage, stillbirth, pre-term delivery, or low infant birth weight."

Wonderful.

I run a hand through my hair. If I don't look a mess, I sure as hell feel like a walking disaster.

"How do we treat Ace Fever?" I ask. "Is there something we can give her? Antibiotics?" I can't even consider that she and the baby may die. That isn't an option.

The doctor pushes his spectacles farther up his nose.

"She will require antibiotic treatment for the infection."

Antibiotics. Thank heaven for modern medicine. "But she'll be all right? She and the baby will make a full recovery?" That's what I need to hear.

"Yes, I believe that she will be fine, but we will have to keep a close eye on the pregnancy. And if the antibiotics don't work and she continues to have symptoms, call me right away. There are rare instances where it can turn into Chronic Ace Fever which may pose a bigger risk."

————

I finally feel like I can breathe again. Moreno is stopping by the local pharmacy with the prescription for Nikki.

While we're not out of the woods, just knowing that she will be fine is a relief.

I just hope the little one growing inside of her can handle the infection and the antibiotic treatment.

I bring a tray into Nikki's bedroom with crackers, soup, and a tall glass of water filled to the brim. It's well after lunch, and she hasn't eaten since breakfast. Given that she hasn't eaten much all week, I'm grateful she managed to stomach toast and jam.

But she can't live off toast while pregnant. She needs a healthy diet.

"What did the doctor say?" Nikki asks. She lies on her side, staring out the window.

"A course of antibiotics will do the trick."

She rolls onto her back, casting a glance at me. Her dark hair splays across the pillow, and she runs her hand over her abdomen. "And the baby?"

I won't lie to her. Already, there are too many lies our pseudo-relationship is built upon. I don't know what else to call it. She's here because I demand her to be, not because she desires to be with me.

Maybe one day that will change. At the very least, my priority is the child that is growing inside of her.

"There are always risks but not taking the antibiotics, you and the baby will die." There's no sugar coating the graveness of the situation. I want her to take it seriously. Not that I doubt that she will, but she and that child, my child, are my responsibility.

She sits up in bed, props herself up with the pillows behind her. I bring the silver tray to the bedside table and place it down for her to reach.

I'm not sure whether I should stay or not.

"Am I contagious?"

"No," I answer.

She rolls her eyes and smirks. "Then sit." Nikki gestures to space on the bed beside her. It's an invitation, and I should take it. I also should be buried in my office working. There's more to be done and surveillance videos to watch.

I oblige her request and perch myself on the edge of her bed. "Eat," I command. If I'm doing as she asks, then she will do as I tell her.

Her eyes glance over at the tray, but she doesn't reach for any of it, not even the crackers.

"Do I have to feed you?" I ask. If she's going to behave like a child, then I will treat her like one.

She reaches for the crackers and brings one to her lips, taking the tiniest nibble. I'm not sure it should even count as eating, but I let it go.

30

NICOLE

I don't trust Dante. How can I, when just yesterday I was at the hospital and doing fine, and then this morning he shows me a video telling me that I'm going to die?

The video is fake. It has to have been manipulated.

His men could have easily created the video and somehow switched identities to make it look like my papa.

I know Papa. He may be harsh and cruel at times, but he would never hurt me, his only daughter.

And the doctor. He works for Dante and would do anything ordered of him, including drugging his patient.

When the pills come, I won't take them. That will be a fight for later. I can tongue the drugs and flush them when no one is watching.

I take a few sips of water after nibbling on crackers to suffice Dante. The last thing I want is for him to force me to eat, but I'm not hungry.

How can he expect me to want to eat after what he's told me?

He stands from the mattress, and I let him leave.

"I'll be back later to check on you," Dante says. He presses a kiss on my forehead.

I try not to flinch.

Dante steps out of my room and shuts the door. I don't hear the click of the lock.

I hurry out of bed and dress for the day.

There are footsteps on the opposite side of the door, just outside the hallway. Voices are muffled behind the thick walls.

Is Dante talking to one of the guards?

Are they discussing me?

I swallow the rest of the glass of water. I'm more thirsty than hungry, but I don't want Dante to feel any hint of satisfaction that I've managed to get fluids or food in me.

If he cares at all, it's about the baby that I'm carrying. He doesn't give a damn about me.

There's a sharp knock at the door, and I race back toward the bed.

"Your medicine," Dante says, showing me the bag from the pharmacy. He opens the stapled paper bag, tearing the top and flipping it upside down to drop the pill bottle onto the mattress.

I reach for the bottle, but he snatches it before I can examine the prescription.

He reads over the instructions and then hands me a pill.

I reach for the nearly empty water glass, and he takes it to the bathroom sink to fill. "You'll need to drink a full glass of water with each dose."

"What did the doctor prescribe?" I ask, reaching for the pill bottle.

Doxycycline.

I've never heard of it specifically, but it sounds legitimate, like an antibiotic.

He wouldn't give me a pill to make me miscarry, would he?

"Here." Dante hands me the glass of water. "The instructions also say it could upset your stomach. I'll have our chef, Savino, prepare you something to eat. Do you think you can stomach lunch?"

"Toast would be good," I say. I doubt I can tolerate much else.

"Take your pill," Dante says. He's standing over me, hovering.

I pretend to put the pill into my mouth, palming the drug into my hand while I down the glass of water.

His eyes narrow.

He doesn't know.

He couldn't know.

Dante grabs my hand and opens my fist. The pill tumbles to the sheets beneath me.

Shit.

His eyes are darker than I've ever seen them as he lifts the pill from the sheets. "Do you have a death wish? Maybe you don't care what happens to my child, but I do," he snarls and grabs my chin.

I pull back, but he doesn't let me loose.

I want to tell him to get off me, but he's holding my bottom jaw open. I don't appreciate being handled.

"Take your damned pill." He shoves it into my mouth and shuts my lips. "Swallow!" he commands.

I swallow, but the pill is still on my tongue. It's bitter and forces my face to scrunch. I want to open my mouth for my glass of water, which is empty.

"Open your mouth."

I roll the pill around in my mouth to shove it in the pocket between my teeth and my jaw. If he demands I lift my tongue, he won't see the stupid drug he's forcing me to take.

When I don't do as he tells me fast enough, he yanks my mouth open. His fingers explore my lips and mouth with one hand while the other keeps my jaw firm.

A visual inspection isn't enough for him.

I try to bite down, but he grabs my tongue.

Bastard!

His index finger swipes between my gums, discovering the pill.

"Moreno!" Dante shouts for his second.

I'm fucked.

Moreno hurries into my bedroom. Had he sensed the urgency in Dante's tone?

"She isn't taking her medicine," Dante says. The wet and sticky pill that has started to dissolve is between his fingers.

"I don't like pills." It's a lie, but I'm willing to try anything to get the two goons to back off.

My lie doesn't work.

"Do you want to hold her down, or I do it, boss?" Moreno asks.

Dante climbs onto the bed and pushes me onto my back. He takes command. He's forceful and not the least bit kind or gentle with his rough movements.

His hips have me pinned down, and I try to ignore the fact his crotch is nestled against my heated core.

He grabs my arms and pins me down, both of my hands held above my head.

There's no reason for him to hold me down, other than the fact he can. He's showing me he's in charge. He could just have easily dropped the pill into a glass of water and forced me to choke it down.

He wants me to see that he is in control.

Moreno holds my jaw open, and Dante, with his single digit, brings the pill into my mouth.

I arch my back struggling to fight Dante, not wanting to take his stupid drug.

With his body pressed tight to mine, all I feel is his heat and smell his savage scent. He's an animal, and I'm his toy to play with and do with whatever he pleases.

My neck is dipped back, making it easier to swallow, and Dante forces the wet and dissolving pill down before I can spit it out.

I cough and gag. The taste is sour, and it melts in the back of my throat, burning on its way down as I swallow to get rid of the bitterness and tingling sensation.

Dante climbs off my frame and stands, shaking his head. "I was going to let you outside, into the garden. You'll have to earn your freedom."

"Freedom?" I sit and push my legs over the side of the bed. "Going outside with guards watching my every move and locked inside your fence isn't freedom."

He tightens his lips but doesn't respond.

Why do I think he would?

Moreno quietly stalks to the bathroom with my empty glass of water and refills it. He brings it back to the bedside table before taking a step back and retreating to the hallway.

He's wise to leave.

At least he can. I'm stuck in my tower like a princess and he's the villain.

Dante steps closer, invading my personal space. He traps me against the bed, but this time he's standing, not pinning me down. My body reacts to his presence. Again.

I don't want to feel the electricity sizzle between us. If it were up to me, I'd feel nothing.

"You have no idea all I've done for you," Dante seethes.

My gaze falls to his lips and then his neck. His black dress shirt is unbuttoned just enough to reveal a glimpse of his chest, and I can't help but stare.

Mentally, I'm undressing him.

I shouldn't be.

He's off-limits—bad news.

And I need to focus on getting my ass away from this prison.

But all I want is for him to kiss me.

Worship me.

Command me.

And remind me that I'm his and his alone. Is that asking too much?

His finger lifts my jaw to look up into his dark gaze. The anger has disappeared, and Dante leans down, brushing his lips across mine.

His kiss is rough.

His touch is forceful as he pushes me back down onto the mattress, straddling my hips.

Just minutes ago, we were in this same position, and while he had overpowered me and angered me, now I only feel warm and calm.

His kisses have the power to bring me down to my knees.

His authority scares me. Not because of who he is or what he does, but because of how it makes me feel. I should hate Dante. I want to hate him.

I also want him to fuck me.

What is wrong with me?

His lips trail along my neck, and his fingers are fast and rough as he lifts my shirt and works the button on my pants free.

The bedroom door is wide open, but Dante doesn't seem to care. Maybe he likes knowing he can claim me in front of his men?

The thought sends a shudder of excitement flowing through my body.

Already, I'm wet.

"I should punish you," Dante rasps into my ear. He flips me over and yanks my jeans down over my bottom.

"Punish me, how?" I'm almost afraid to ask. He's already forced me to swallow that stupid pill.

"Get on all fours," he commands and lifts my hips.

I do as I'm told. The zipper on his pants glides down, and I glance over my shoulder. I want to see him.

His cock is glistening and hard. Dante strokes his thickened member and shoves my head forward, bending my head down as he thrusts hard inside of my tightness.

A whimper slips out past my lips.

It doesn't hurt. He fills me and makes me feel full as he stretches my insides to accommodate him. Each thrust is slow and drawn out.

It's pure torture.

"Harder," I whisper, needing more and wanting him to go faster.

He doesn't listen to me. Each stroke is slow and deliciously painful.

My insides throb and pulsate around his thick cock.

"Please," I beg. My hands bunch into fists as the bedsheets are all that I can grasp.

Dante pushes my head down against the bed as he fucks me.

Finally, he gives me what I want. The pace picks up, and my heart is slamming against my ribcage.

My insides clench down.

"Not yet!" Dante commands. "Don't you dare come yet."

"Fuck," I mutter under my breath. Already, I'm so close, and he's teasing me to no end.

He pulls out just as I reach the edge.

I gasp, and my breath feels stolen from my lungs.

"What the fuck was that?" I'm panting, desperate for air, and he flips me around onto my back.

There's a devious smile that crosses his features, and a dark glint in his eye. "You're mine," he growls and lifts my legs to his shoulders as he drives himself into me.

It's hard and rough, and my insides are pulsating all over again.

"Please," I beg, not wanting him to pull away from me again. I'm tinkering on the edge of oblivion, clenching and trying to make the moment last.

"Tell me I'm all yours, and you can come."

I moan as the lingering sensation of warmth builds into sparks like the first sizzle of fireworks before they're launched across the sky. "Dante," I plead with him.

His movements are slow.

I'm delirious.

It's killing me.

"I'm yours. All yours." He can do whatever he pleases with me right here. Right now.

"Good girl." His thrusts quicken and slam against me as he drives deeper into my heat.

I'm right there on the edge, not even pretending to silence the impending orgasm as it rips through my body like fire burning in intensity as he plows into me.

One.

Two.

Three more strokes, and he's spilling himself inside my warmth as my insides pulse and clench down, pulling him tighter, harder, closer.

My heart and our labored breathing are all I hear as he rolls off and onto the bed beside me.

31

DANTE

I want to scream at Nicole. The anger flows through me and burns like an inferno.

What the hell is wrong with her?

Why would she pretend to take her medicine? After all I've done to protect her, and she still believes I'm the monster.

That's not to say I'm a saint.

I'm not. I've killed men.

But even I have a line I wouldn't cross, and that's hurting an innocent woman—especially one who's pregnant with my child.

Does she not realize that I don't intend to hurt her? I'm keeping her here for her protection.

Her father was willing to poison her, torture her, and sell her in a bid to marry any man for the right price.

There's a baby growing inside of her.

My baby.

I shift onto my side and rest my hand over her abdomen. She barely appears to be showing, but she also hasn't eaten much since she's arrived.

I need to do better.

If that means forcing her to eat, so be it. Whatever it takes to make sure my son or daughter is healthy. Even if Nikki hates me for it, what other choice is there?

A heavy silence falls over the room before I finally push myself off the mattress and pull my clothes back on. My men don't need to see my bare ass or anything else, even if we did leave the door wide open.

Good.

Let them know she's mine.

She's off-limits to any man who so much as looks at her.

I'll kill him.

My men know better than to betray me. But it didn't stop me from claiming her with the door wide open for any of my men to witness.

"Get dressed," I command.

Nikki doesn't move from the bed. Her hair is fanned out across the silken white sheets. She looks angelic.

She's anything but an angel. Her father is Gino DeLuca.

And yet, I let her into my home. I protected her. Ravaged her.

The appreciation I get is null.

Void.

Nothing.

"Get up!" I'm tired of her ignoring me. I'm the fucking king of this castle and the family. She will listen to me. Obey me. And do as I command.

Her breath catches in her throat, and she climbs out of bed, bringing the sheets with her. Like I didn't just see and mark every ounce of her naked flesh.

Since when is she shy?

Is it an act? I watch her scurry to pick up her clothes and rush into the bathroom.

There's still no door, and I can see every inch of her body, but I pretend not to care. Like her nakedness means nothing to me when all I want to do is throw her back down on the bed and fuck her again.

One look at her, and I grow hard.

I wait by the open bedroom door and shift on my feet. She is an impossible distraction. Nikki will get me killed if I'm not careful.

But I know it's worth it.

She's worth it.

She's thrown on the t-shirt that she wore earlier, but it's obvious she's not wearing a bra.

I shut my jaw, trying not to stare.

Her jeans hug her curves in every delicious way possible. She saunters out of the bathroom, not looking the least bit like she's just been fucked.

How the hell does she do it? Toy with my heart and my cock.

"I'm dressed," she says and gestures toward the clothes that she's wearing.

"Good. I'm taking you outside to the garden."

Moreno is right. A pregnant woman needs sunshine and, more importantly, vitamin D.

Her bottom lip tugs between her teeth, and she follows me out of the bedroom. I leave the door open. There's no sense in closing it or keeping anyone else out.

My hand falls to her lower back, finding the perfect spot to sit as I lead her down the stairwell and through the kitchen.

There's a back door, an entrance that leads directly to the garden. It has a small fence, one that could easily be climbed, but there's a taller gate just outside, with guards at the post and along the property line.

She's not going anywhere, even if she tries to run.

"I thought you could use some sunshine," I say as I open the door and let her step out first.

"Are you telling me I'm pasty?"

She's tentative at first, with one foot and then the other as she steps out onto the stone pavers.

Is it disbelief?

I follow her outside and close the door behind us. There's no sense in letting the air conditioning outside.

Her shoulders fall, and her head dips back, eyes closed, basking in the bright warmth of the sun shining overhead. The sky is blue without so much as a cloud above or along the horizon.

Stepping around her, I stalk off toward the wooden bench and have a seat. There are flowers growing along the fence line for decoration, but most of the interior of the garden has vegetables and herbs for cooking and preparing meals.

I sit on the bench and study her. The corner of her lips curl in a faint smile. She appears blissful, almost happy.

My intent was never to keep her here, locked up in my home.

But she's pregnant with my child. What other option is there?

After several minutes, she comes to sit beside me on the bench. Her fingers are tucked at the edge of the wood, gripping the seat. "Thank you," she whispers.

"I'd like to think that I can trust you, Nicole."

She shivers, and I can't tell if it's involuntary, or she's cold. The sun feels warm, but I also have a button-down shirt on and am dressed for the day, for business.

"Please, call me Nikki. Only Papa calls me Nicole." Her voice is distant, her eyes fixated on the flowers. Or maybe it's the small fence several feet away at the edge of the garden.

There's something about the way she says Nicole, the way her nose scrunches and her bottom lip juts out that insinuates she doesn't like it.

"Nikki, I'd like to trust you. We're inevitably tied together from now on, with that baby growing inside of you. My baby," I say.

I brush a strand of her dark curls behind her ear.

"A baby shouldn't grow up without two parents. And your father. It was with his blessing that we marry."

32

NICOLE

"What?" I swear my eyes bug out of my head, and I jump from my seat on the bench outside in the garden.

Did he seriously just propose?

"That was the worst proposal in the history of proposals," I say.

And since when did he speak with Papa about marrying me? Does he know I'm pregnant?

"Well, I didn't exactly plan any of this, in case you haven't noticed." Dante is quick with a comeback.

I fold my arms across my chest. "You don't want to marry me." There are a dozen reasons I can think that this is a terrible idea. Does he want me to reel them off?

"I don't want my child not knowing his father, and I'm pretty sure the first opportunity you get, you're going to split."

I laugh under my breath. Does he believe a ring is going to change that or a bunch of vows and a piece of paper?

"No. I won't marry you. I'll never marry you." He's crazy if he thinks I want to be here, with him, forever. "In case you've forgotten, I'm your prisoner, Dante."

His jaw is tight, and his lips are in a firm line as he stares at me. "You're treated like a princess. Not like a prisoner. Do you want to see my basement where I hold men who steal from me?"

My mouth goes dry.

"Is that what this is about? Your stupid truck I stole." I can't believe he hasn't let that go. I didn't know who he was or I wouldn't have risked pissing him off.

"No, it's about the fact I bought you from your father."

Did I hear him correctly? "What?" I ask.

No.

I couldn't have heard what he said. Or rather, he didn't mean it like it came out.

Shaking my head, I take a step back, the edge of my feet against the wood planks containing the vegetables behind me.

"You're lying." Whatever he intends to say, I don't believe him. I can't believe him. Because otherwise, it would mean the absolute worst thing imaginable, that my father was behind my abduction.

That can't be true.

Papa wouldn't have me kidnapped, abducted, humiliated, and sold.

"No," I say, shaking my head in dismay.

It's the only word I can say. The only word that I keep chanting over and over again because I don't want to believe it.

I can't believe it.

"I swore to him I wouldn't tell you," Dante seethes. He stands and paces on the pavers, his feet stomping over the bricks, each thud clunky and heavy with his weight and anger pouring out of him.

"I can't, Dante, I just, I can't—" I say and rush for the door to the kitchen.

I can't hear his excuses.

I don't want to hear it, to believe it. None of it can be true because if it is, I don't know where I fit into this world anymore.

He doesn't chase me.

Or if he does, I'm quicker than he is and don't hear him following me.

I rush through the kitchen and then down the hallway to the foyer. I snag a pair of shoes left by the door. They're two sizes too big, but I don't care. I slip on the shiny black men's shoes and tear outside.

One of the guards says something to me, but I don't hear him. It's all a blur, a whirlwind as I run for the gate.

My feet crunch over gravel and then through the grass. The metal iron gates are high and pointed, dangerous to climb.

"Please," I beg, as I run for the locked entrance.

What makes me think they'll let me go?

Why would I think he'd ever give me freedom?

The guard at the gate picks up the phone as I approach.

"Yes, sir," the guard says and clicks the buzzer unlocking the gate.

It's slow to open, but I don't care. I slip past after it widens just a few inches, enough to let me free. I can't take a chance that he'll reconsider and drag me back.

33

DANTE

"Open the gate," I say to the guard standing at the post.

From the front window, I watch Nikki leave. She scoots out past the wrought iron and runs.

How far will she get?

Where will she go? Back to her father who poisoned her?

Moreno walks over toward me, and I swear he's wearing a smug smile behind his façade.

"Don't say a word," I warn. I'm not in the mood to deal with his bullshit or anyone else's today.

"We can go to the club, find a nice pretty girl to take your mind off her," he suggests.

I huff under my breath. "That's what got me into this damned mess."

He was there. Moreno ought to remember the night I met Nikki. Although he did a decent job of pretending not to notice Nikki and me fucking in my club.

"I want a pair of eyes on her at all times," I say. "It's for her own protection."

Moreno doesn't question my motives. He knows better and gives a sharp nod. "On it. You want me to send one of our soldiers?"

"I want you to do it," I say. With heavy footfalls, I stomp into my office.

My head is spinning, and I'm about ready to puke.

Why the hell did I let her go? What was I thinking?

I unbutton the top two buttons on my dress shirt. Sweat trickles across my forehead. My shirt is suffocating.

Hell, this room is suffocating.

"Boss, she'll recognize me."

He isn't wrong. Nikki has spent enough time around Moreno to know that I sent him to follow her.

"Good." I'm not hiding the fact that we're keeping tabs on her. She left with my child growing inside of her.

He exhales a loud sigh. "You know I'd do anything you asked of me, boss. I just want to state that this is a bad idea."

In my office, on the long wooden cabinet against the wall, there's a decanter with whiskey. I flip over a glass and pour the amber liquid.

"Noted." I don't care what he thinks. Maybe I should. He is the one person I trust to be honest with me, blatantly so. But at the end of the day, I'm the one who makes the rules and enforces them.

I swirl the liquid around the edge of the glass before downing it in one gulp. The burn as it glides down my throat is the only satisfaction that I get today.

"What are you waiting for?" I shoot over my shoulder, not so much as turning around to look at him.

"Right. I'll report back on her whereabouts," Moreno says. He tears out of the office.

Will she steal another vehicle in her effort to escape?

I run a hand through my hair before pouring a second glass of whiskey—the pangs of anger rip at my gut.

Why did I let her go?

I down the drink and throw the glass across the room. It shatters as it hits the wall and descends onto the floor into tiny shards.

With it, my heart splinters.

Nikki is gone.

Defeat crushes me but doesn't hold me down.

I'll bring her back, even if she's kicking and screaming.

34

NICOLE

It feels surreal, escape.

Except, is it escape when your captor unlocks the gate and lets you go?

Why did he let me leave? Did Dante realize that I wasn't his and would never be his? What did he mean he bought me from my father?

No, it was a trick. It had to be a manipulation tactic used to instill fear and distrust.

Well, I sure as shit don't trust Dante.

I'm still not sure why he let me leave. Maybe it was a moment of weakness. Either way, it doesn't matter.

I hurry along the path through the forest and cut across the mountainside, heading toward town. I follow the trail and keep a steady pace.

Every so often, I glance over my shoulder. I hear noise in the distance, the rustling of trees and branches. I can't ascertain if it's someone following me or the wind.

It's probably one of Dante's goons.

I grimace as I hurry across the riverbank. My shoes that are too big are now flooded with water.

Great. I can't take them off without scraping the bottoms of my feet, but each step grows louder as my feet slosh around. In the distance, I spot a log cabin and a wooden sign that swings with the wind: Lumberjack Shack.

———

I grab a seat at the counter and nurse my glass of water.

"Can I get you something to eat?" the gentleman behind the counter asks.

I don't have any money. Though, I imagine if I call Papa, he will come to bail my ass out and pay for any food I consume. The truth is that I'm not hungry.

Fight or flight indeed kicked in when I ran.

"Do you have a phone that I can use?" I ask.

The man's eyes narrow just a bit. He's tall with broad shoulders and a thick, bushy beard. If I had to guess, he owns the place.

"Did your car break down?" he asks. "I can have one of my buddies give it a tow."

I sip my water and my mouth still is dry. My lips feel like the desert. "No, I'm just in a bit of a bind." I don't want to elaborate.

Trust is a delicate issue right now, and while he's handsome and easy on the eyes, I spot the wedding band on his hand.

Too bad he's off-limits.

I'm also pregnant.

It's probably the hormones raging through my body making me want to fuck any man with a pulse.

Well, that's not exactly true. I don't want to fuck Dante. At least not again.

Okay, maybe not right now.

"Got it." He smiles warmly and digs out his cell phone from his pocket. "My name's Lincoln, by the way. Just holler at me when you're done." He unlocks his cell phone and hands it over to me.

"Thank you."

I watch him stroll across the restaurant. In the corner booth is a woman in her late twenties, maybe early thirties. I'm terrible with guessing ages, but she's beautiful and strangely familiar.

I'm not sure why. I shouldn't know anyone from this town.

Yet, I feel like I know her.

I've seen her before.

I don't recognize her from the compound where I was held prisoner. At least, I don't think she was there.

She smiles and laughs at Lincoln. The girl is beautiful, gorgeous, and probably won beauty pageants and could have been a model.

Beside her are two little ones.

No, she wasn't at the compound.

She glances up at me and smiles warmly. I feel like I've been caught staring and avert my gaze. I punch in Papa's cell phone and wait for him to pick it up.

"Lincoln, what the hell do you want?" Papa's voice rattles through the phone.

How does he know Lincoln?

"Papa, it's me, Nicole," I say. When I use the name he prefers, a shudder rips through me, the only name he will call me by.

"Nicole, dear. Where are you? Why are you keeping company with slime like Lincoln? Is that who Dante converses with?"

I rub my forehead, frustrated that Papa doesn't take two seconds to worry about me so much as to even ask how I've been. Did he even plan on coming to rescue me or leave me to rot and die with Dante?

"Papa, I need you to send a car to pick me up. I'm at Lumberjack Shack."

He snorts. "Of course, my dear. I will send Vance over soon. Why the hell is my princess with men like that? Those men who Dante consorts with are dangerous, Nicole. Do not trust them."

Before I can say anything further, the line goes dead. Papa ends the call without so much as a goodbye.

I sigh and climb off the stool, pattering with wet shoes over to Lincoln and, I presume, his family.

"Everything okay? Get ahold of who you need?" Lincoln asks.

"Yes, thank you," I say, and hand him his phone.

The woman smiles at Lincoln and hands over the girl to, again, I presume, her husband. She climbs out of the booth and gently guides my arm as she leads me away.

"Are you okay?" she asks. Her voice is soft and gentle, friendly. Her smile appears genuine, and her eyes glint with something I don't quite recognize. Concern? Worry? I'm not sure I've ever recognized that expression without it being etched in fear.

She glances down at my sopping shoes. They're not mine, especially given my attire. "Do you need help?" she offers. "I'm Harper."

I heed Papa's warning. These people aren't to be trusted.

"I'm all right. Your husband, he let me borrow his phone. My family will be here soon to pick me up." I point toward the door. "I can wait outside."

Maybe it would be better if I waited outside and put some distance between these folks. They look kind, but appearances can be deceiving. I learned that the hard way from Dante.

He charmed a baby right into me.

Not that I worry Lincoln or Harper would do the same. They seem happy, pleasant, and maybe in another life, we could have been friends.

But not in this life.

And certainly not today.

The restaurant's door squeaks and swings open. I spin around on my heels and my feet stumble. Harper grabs my elbow and my hip to keep me from hitting the floor.

I want to mumble thanks, but not even those words come out when I stare at the man entering the diner.

What the hell is Moreno doing here?

I shrug out of the woman's grasp.

"You should go," I whisper. I'm not sure if I'm saying it to Harper or Moreno. The words fill the air, and she takes a step back and hurries toward where she was seated earlier.

"What the hell are you doing in here, Moreno?" Lincoln swiftly hands his little girl back to Harper and storms toward the door to confront him.

I'm speechless that they know each other, and they don't appear on the best terms. I thought there were only two feuding mafia families in Breckenridge. Lincoln isn't part of the DeLuca family and doesn't appear to be on good terms with the Riccis, either.

"Just coming for the food."

"The hell you are!" Lincoln points toward the door. "You're not welcome. I spent months having the place remodeled because of men like you," Lincoln seethes.

Moreno gives a sideways smirk. "That might be, but it wasn't my men who tore apart your business. Those bastards don't work for my boss, and I don't work for you. I've got orders, and I'm following them."

His eyes stay on me, and Lincoln's gaze quickly follows.

"Oh, for fuck's sake." He throws his hands up into the air. "She's one of yours?" His cheeks burn red.

"I'm not anyone's," I say, but it's not like either of them hear me. I may as well be invisible.

35

DANTE

"What do you mean you lost her?" I clutch my cell phone to my ear as I pace the hallway outside my office.

I can't seem to sit still long enough to get any amount of work done. I've been this way since I let her leave.

"Vance picked her up. I'm guessing she called Daddy Dearest," Moreno says.

That's all I need to hear. My feet pound the floor, and I toss open the door to my office. I hit the light switch, and my eyes squint from the bright, blinding halogen overhead lights. I should have them replaced.

I slump into my chair behind my desk and yank out the tablet that is wired to the video surveillance at DeLuca's place.

Leaning back in my chair, one hand clings to the tablet and the other to my phone. "Well, she's not home yet."

I flip through a half dozen screens with multiple angles and viewpoints inside and out of Gino's property. I should get a decent view of her arrival, if that's where Vance is taking her.

A pit forms in my stomach.

What if they send her back to the compound and terrorize her all over again?

Thinking such horrid thoughts will only cause me unnecessary concern. If it wasn't for my child that she's carrying, I'm not sure that I'd be quite so adamant about chasing after her.

Is that the only reason I want her here, with me?

"I'm tailing Vance, but it looks like they're heading back to Gino's," Moreno says.

"Come back to the compound. There's no sense in you following them any farther." I keep a watchful eye on the tablet, scrolling between screens, just in case there's something worthy of investigating.

"Sure thing, boss."

I end the call, and the phone tumbles with a thud onto my desk. It takes every ounce of strength not to throw it across the room.

My fingers itch with anger and anxiety. I ball my hands into fists and exhale loudly through my nose.

The office is hot.

Stuffy.

With two hands, I grip the tablet, staring at the screen and the multiple camera angles from different nearby locations at the DeLuca property.

The only room that has a wire is Gino's office, and it's empty.

I flit through the video footage, looking for anything that could give me an advantage.

Gino stands on the porch, his arms folded across his chest. He's waiting for Nikki to arrive home.

I flip through two more camera feeds and catch sight of the gate opening. Behind it, an SUV waits to enter.

I can't see the driver, let alone who else is in the vehicle, but I surmise it's Nikki, and soon enough, I'll know without a doubt.

The SUV halts abruptly at the front entrance, and the passenger door of the vehicle swings open. The video flickers but comes back as quickly as it glitched.

Nikki climbs out of the SUV and is standing in front of her father. He's taller than she is, even more so with him standing on the step just above her.

Her shoulders are slouched and her head down. I can't read her lips, let alone see them from my current angle.

There are no hugs. No warm greetings from what I can make out. The video is top notch, but it's still not perfect. There's sunlight interfering, and their positioning doesn't give me any advantage, either.

Gino points at the entrance of the door, and I swear she's stomping inside.

Maybe it's all in my head, and I imagine the sassiness that sizzles right off of her.

I flip through the video feeds and glance up when I hear footsteps approach my office.

Moreno steps into my office and shuts the door behind him.

I barely make eye contact with him.

"She's just a girl. There are plenty more of them out there," Moreno says.

I balk at his suggestion.

"She's carrying my child. I shouldn't have let her go." I slam my fist against the wooden desk. Anger boils my blood, running through my veins.

The last thing I need is to appear weak. Letting her leave was a mistake, one that I have to fix.

I fucked up.

Big time.

I drop the tablet on the desk and stand.

"What's the plan?" Moreno asks. He's already one step ahead. We've worked together closely for so long that he has the uncanny ability to know what I'm thinking. "We break into the DeLuca's compound and kidnap her?"

When he says it like that, it sounds horrible, but she's mine, and that baby is mine. I can't let anything happen to the child she's carrying.

"Her father poisoned her," I say and throw my hands into the air. "The way I see it, we're mounting a rescue mission."

Moreno cocks a grin. "Any way you want to see it, boss. Suddenly we're the good guys." He laughs under his breath.

Yeah, crazy.

36

NICOLE

"Papa." I climb out of the SUV and head for the entrance.

He's standing over me on the top step, towering above. His arms are folded across his broad chest, and he doesn't seem the least bit pleased to see me.

Why is that?

I know I left in a huff and technically ran away, but that feels like ages ago. He saw me that night when I'd been kidnapped.

Wasn't he worried about me being forced to go home with Dante?

"You are a disgrace to the family," Papa says.

I don't apologize. I bite down on my tongue to keep my lips sealed and my thoughts contained.

"Do you know the trouble that you've caused? The hours of manpower to handle you and your drama?" Papa scolds.

Does that mean if I'd have held out a little longer at Dante's that Papa would have eventually come for me?

The tongue lashing continues.

"I expect that while you're under my roof, you will abide by my rules, Nicole. First, you will go up to your room and pretty yourself up. While you may have thought you've gotten out of one marriage, I can attest to the fact that you will be wed."

"What?" I can't keep quiet any longer. "Papa, no!" Has he lost his mind?

He points toward the door. "Inside and upstairs. Now!" His voice sends an involuntary shiver through me.

I'm practically thrust into the house, my shoes clomping the floor as I storm up the stairs to my bedroom.

I slam the bedroom door and feel the house vibrate.

It's like I'm twelve all over again and being punished for sneaking out. I toss off the shoes that are Dante's or one of his men's. I'm not sure, and I don't give a rat's ass.

They'll end up in the trash later.

I sit at the edge of the bed and fall back onto the mattress, my legs dangling over the side.

Coming here was a mistake.

My heart aches and my stomach is a bundle of knots, but there are no tears, only years of anger buried deep within me, ready and willing to seep out.

I don't budge from my position on the bed. I'm not quite locked in my bedroom like I was with Dante, but there's nowhere for me to go without being reprimanded. Especially tonight.

There's a firm rap at the bedroom door.

"Come in," I say.

Papa wouldn't knock. He'd just barge right in.

Vance opens the bedroom door and steps into the room. He glances over his shoulder at me. "Your father asked me to check on you." He holds up a finger to wait, and then he closes the door behind him.

I'm not up for his antics or games. Vance is Papa's second in command. He's as loyal as they come. Practically a dog that follows him around with an eagerness to please.

I sit up, giving him my attention, but that's all he gets. "I'm not marrying anyone."

I'm not the least bit thrilled to be back.

This was my doing. I had the opportunity to flee and start over, and I should have taken it.

"You should shower and get dressed. He'll be here for dinner, and you never know, you might actually like him," Vance says.

He's good with people and knows how to win the hearts of many ladies.

But he can't convince me to play ball in his court.

"Here's an idea. Why don't you go in my place?" I quip.

"Snarky isn't your color," Vance shoots back.

I give a mild shrug and stretch my arms. "I'm not going to dinner with some guy Papa sets me up with." There is no chance that he can convince me. Besides, I'm not hungry. I haven't been in quite some time.

The thought of food and having to play nice with some male stranger rattles me and turns my stomach.

Or maybe it's the pregnancy or that stupid fever Dante told me that I was infected with.

Either way, any second, I'm about to be sick.

I leap from the bed and tear across the room for the connecting bathroom. I slam the door shut, hit the fan, and lift the lid.

I pray Vance doesn't follow me or ask questions. He can believe it's food poisoning or nerves. I don't give a shit which he falls for, but I'm not entertaining one of Papa's clients.

"You can't hide in there forever," Vance shouts at me and knocks on the door.

"Yes, I can. Go away!"

Quietness follows for several drawn-out minutes.
Maybe he hears me vomiting, or he decided to give
me some space. I doubt he will cut me any slack.

He'll be back.

I finish in the bathroom and stumble back to bed,
lying above the freshly made covers. The sheets are
tucked tight, and I yank the comforter hard to climb
beneath it. I don't care that the curtains are open and
it's the middle of the afternoon.

I'm exhausted.

I doze off. I'm not sure for how long when I hear the
heavy lead of shoes stomping a path up the stairs,
down the hall, and toward my room.

It's loud enough to wake the dead.

Fuck.

Papa rips my door open, the handle breaking off in
his hand.

It didn't take much honestly. The screws were loose,
and the handle was cheap and needed repair.

"I don't care whether you want to join Romano for
dinner or not. You will accompany him and be

dressed appropriately. If you can't handle that, I will have Vance bathe you, dress you, and I will escort you as a chaperone."

"You won't send Vance as my chaperone?"

Papa's answer is dry. There's no smile or glint in his eye. "No," he says.

I've disappointed him. It's obvious, and I wouldn't care except if I'm going to stay here, then I need to find a way to convince him to let me be.

Do I tell him about the baby? Is that my ticket to escape his madness? He wants to marry me off.

Why? For his empire or some other reason that I can't even comprehend?

His ideas have always been antiquated. I never thought much of it until I went away to college. It's too bad I came home. That was the biggest mistake of my life.

Next to coming back here.

And the baby.

Well, okay, that makes three.

I don't make good decisions.

It's not like I was raised in a stable family with a normal childhood. My father was in the mafia, and while he wasn't don, he climbed the ranks quickly. That doesn't happen by being kind or empathetic.

He's a killer.

I'm not an idiot. I know what he's done, but it doesn't mean he has to ship me off and marry me to the highest bidder.

"Do you have nothing to say for yourself, Nicole?" He's waiting for an apology, or at least a word of acceptance.

He wants my defeat.

Well, he won't get it.

"I can't marry Romano," I say. I know exactly what will anger Papa—telling him the truth.

I'd rather he kick me to the curb, toss me out, instead of forcing me to marry a stranger.

Exhaling a nervous breath, I let the words free. "I'm pregnant."

There's no hint of emotion, and the anger I was expecting is well hidden if it exists at all. Papa has learned to channel his emotions mostly into anger.

I'm also well versed in his disappointment in me.

Papa holds up a hand to indicate that he's heard enough. "Get showered, dressed, and ready for Romano to join you for dinner."

"Are we going out?" I ask. If Papa lets me leave with Romano, then there's a chance I can escape on foot. Or steal another vehicle. This time, though, I won't get caught.

His eyes tighten as he watches me. "Leave? No, you're not to be trusted outside of these four walls until you're wed."

The air is stolen from my lungs. "What?" He can't be serious. He wouldn't hold me as a prisoner, would he?

"I'm tired of your childish antics, Nicole. You will marry Romano."

I wish Mamma was still around. She was the only person who could stand up to him, although he hadn't been particularly kind to her, either.

"I'm to marry him, even if I don't love him?"

"Love is a notion created by men with deep pockets."

I approach the window, my only bit of sanctuary while locked inside. I stare out at the garden in the middle of the compound. Even if I could break free, open my window, and climb down, there's nowhere to flee.

"I can't marry Romano. I'm in love with Dante, and I'm having his child," I say. My hand falls to my abdomen. I'm barely showing, and the clothes I wear fit loose enough that no one can tell.

Papa storms farther into the bedroom, cornering me at the window. "Do you want a fatherless child? A son or daughter to grow up with no role model. That's what you're asking of me, Nicole, to let you live in a fantasy world where you raise a child on your own."

Would Dante want to raise the baby with me? It's not something that we had discussed.

"I wouldn't be on my own. I'd have Dante."

I've lost my mind.

That's the only reason I could be saying such insane things to Papa. It's easier to believe Dante would want to marry me than to accept the harsh reality of marrying Romano.

"Then why did you leave Dante? You were to wed him, and you ran away. Same as you always do, Nicole. You don't know what you want. You're practically a child," Papa says and stares down at me. He pats the top of my head like one would with a little kid.

It makes my stomach flip.

I force his arm away.

He's belittling me, demeaning, and I hate it.

I hate him.

The anger roils through me, clouding my mind. What did he say about marrying Dante? "What do you mean I was to wed him?"

I'm glad to be seated at the edge of the pristine white windowsill. The view of the garden below is mildly calming as I tear my gaze away from Papa. I need space, but he doesn't give me any. Being in his presence is smothering.

That was how I felt with Dante, except different.

I can't explain it.

Dante may have kept me locked in his tower, but he genuinely appeared to care about me. But then again, he had abducted me and forced me to live with him.

My fingers tangle through my hair.

I swear I need professional help, but who could I talk to? I mean, my father and the father of my child are both mafia don's. Our lives and everything we witness are sworn to secrecy.

Therapy isn't an exemption.

"This conversation is done," Papa says.

Good.

I'm tired of dealing with him too.

Does that mean that I won?

"You have an hour to get ready before Romano arrives."

I'll just have to make him not want me. How hard can that be? Worst case, I tell Romano I'm pregnant. That ought to scare him off.

37

DANTE

"There's a truck pulling into the compound," Sawyer says over the earpiece. He's one of my capos.

I've brought in nearly all my men and left only a few soldiers behind to guard our fort.

"Any sign of who or what is inside?" I ask.

It's no secret that Gino is involved in arms deals, girls, and drugs. Two out of three, I see little issue with, but women, including children, hell no.

I have some morals.

"A guy in a suit just parked and is exiting his truck. I don't recognize him," Moreno says. He's hunched beside me with binoculars, surveying the scene.

I hold out my hand. I want to see this douche bag who works for Gino.

I don't recognize him. I hand the binoculars back to Moreno and glance down at the tablet that I brought. We're connected to Wi-Fi through the phone towers, so we're getting a decent signal, and I can keep an eye on their surveillance and make sure that no one is coming unexpectedly.

"Boss," Sawyer's voice cracks through the earpiece. The audio signal is having issues, but the video is still pristine.

I hold out a finger to Moreno to wait, and then the line comes back, crystal clear. "You wouldn't believe this. The suit brought flowers, a bouquet of roses, to the compound. Who the fuck brings the don flowers?"

"It's not for Gino," I state, my mouth dry. "Whoever it is, he's here for Nikki."

I doubt there's an entourage of women receiving flowers at the DeLuca compound. There may be several ladies being held captive, but no one is wooing them.

A guy only buys flowers for a girl when he's trying to fuck her or in the doghouse and apologizing.

I'm glad I didn't waste another minute at home.

Am I impulsive? Probably, but I don't give a shit.

Nikki is mine.

No one else is getting near Nikki or my baby.

Certainly not some suit with roses.

Fuck that. I can't survey any longer.

"How many guards along the perimeter?" We need to move before the situation becomes dire.

Sawyer's voice comes on the line first. "We've got two guards at the north entrance. I can create a diversion on the east side and draw them away."

"Wait," Caden, another capo, interrupts before Sawyer can follow through on his plan.

"Gino just stepped outside. I've got the shot. I can take him out," Caden says.

Nikki is the priority, but the opportunity to take out the boss of the DeLuca empire is a worthwhile distraction. "Do it," I say.

Gino is a pig, snatching young girls and trafficking them through his enterprise. He won't be missed. Certainly not by me.

From my position, I can't see the hit.

The surveillance footage doesn't show it, either, which is a blessing because at least his men won't know what hit them.

Moreno and I keep an eye on the surveillance footage, giving my men ample time to take out guard after guard before we're caught.

Orders are tossed around, having my men clear the perimeter as we prepare to breach the main entrance. I can't watch the footage and be on the front lines.

Strategically, I should stay behind, but as don, I refuse to order my men to war without stepping foot on the battlefield. I hand over the tablet to Moreno.

He's my second. If anything happens to me, my men will follow his orders.

There's a handgun at my ankle, and a semiautomatic draped around my shoulder. I grip the weapon and remind my men that whatever they do, do not shoot Nikki.

She's carrying my child.

Letting her leave was a mistake. A momentary lapse in judgment. She deserves freedom but not in the same way she thinks she wants it.

Nikki doesn't realize the danger that she's waltzed into by returning home.

Her father poisoned her. He ordered her abduction and allowed her to be sold.

I tried to warn her, but she didn't believe me.

Why would she?

Now I've come to rescue her and my child that she carries.

But will she see it that way?

38

NICOLE

Romano brings me roses. Am I supposed to fall head over heels for his effort?

They were obviously bought at the grocery store.

He couldn't even spare the expense of going to a florist.

I hate roses. They're the color of blood.

My mother had been given a bouquet of red roses on the day she'd been murdered.

Romano couldn't have known about the flowers or my mother's death. At least, I don't think he had any inclination of the two.

I carry the roses to the kitchen and find a vase under the sink. Cutting the stems, I prick my thumb.

Blood oozes into the sink and I run the tap, shoving my thumb underneath the faucet.

"Damn roses," I mutter to myself.

If I was superstitious, I'd think it was an omen.

But I'm not.

Well, usually, I'm not.

My stomach bubbles, and I contemplate it's just my nerves that have me on edge. This is the last place that I want to be, with a stranger, having dinner at the orders of my father.

If he wasn't a mob boss ordering an arranged marriage like a steak at a restaurant, I'd be humiliated. I can find my own date. Hell, if given enough time, I could probably find a husband, too.

Of course, being pregnant doesn't help matters, but I can handle a baby on my own. How hard can it be?

I finish with the roses and take my time sauntering back into the dining room, where Romano waits. He hasn't sat down yet, and he looks awkwardly out of place.

He's pleasant enough, but not really my type. He's short, a bit stocky, and his hair looks like it was dyed with shoe polish. I'll bet anything that the color will rub off on the furniture.

"I hope you like the flowers, Nicole. I made a special trip to town to get them for you."

Am I supposed to be impressed? Because I'm not.

I don't answer Romano. His flowers aren't worth the compliment.

Why does Papa want me to marry him? Is it for a parcel of land and two oxen? This isn't the 1800s. I am not to be paraded around and sold at auction.

Except that was precisely what happened, and Dante owns me.

Did he buy me, or was it his operation all along?

"Your father tells me you've been through quite an ordeal recently," Romano says. He gestures for me to sit down at the table and pulls out my chair.

Is this how he normally acts or is it a show he's putting on, because every so often, Papa walks by the dining room. His footsteps are obvious on his approach.

"Yes." I take a seat at the table. There's a beautiful pristine white tablecloth with lace trim at the edges adorning the table, but the food hasn't been brought out yet.

Papa has a full-time chef who prepares all our meals. I anticipate the same for tonight.

"I suppose I'm lucky that your father sold you to Dante instead of his original plan."

What is he talking about? "Excuse me?"

"You know, his plan to poison you. He warned me that you might not be hungry for dinner and a tad moody because of the antibiotics that they've put you on but has assured me that you aren't contagious."

I'm going to be sick. I rest my hands flat on the table. "Papa sold me to Dante?"

"Yes, he orchestrated the abduction because of your temper tantrum, to teach you a lesson. I hope it worked. I hate to admit that I'm not nearly as creative as your father."

I'm going to kill Papa.

Nausea and dread turn to disgust.

My only choice is to let Romano down as kindly as I can.

I rest my hand over my abdomen. It's now or never. Hopefully, it scares him away.

"Did you hear the news? I'm carrying Dante Ricci's child." I rest a hand over my abdomen with a sly smile.

I half-expect Papa to storm into the dining room and berate me, but he doesn't come.

In fact, his footsteps are no longer heard in the hall. He must have gone to his office or stepped outside for fresh air.

"Don Ricci's child?" Romano asks. His eyes widen, and his skin turns ghastly. He didn't seem bothered by my father poisoning me, abducting me, and selling me, but pregnancy is too much for him.

Maybe he'll stop pretending that he wants to marry me and excuse himself from the table.

I'd much prefer to eat alone.

Gunfire erupts just outside the compound. "Gino's been hit. We're under attack!" Vance's voice carries into the dining room.

Romano pushes out of his chair and grabs his pistol at his hip. "Don't worry. I'll protect you."

That is precisely what I'm worried about.

I push past Romano. I need to see my father.

"Papa!" I shout, expecting Vance to tell me where he is or to hear Papa's groans in agony. He can't be far.

I don't glance over my shoulder at Romano. He has a weapon and can defend himself. Whether he lives or dies isn't any of my concern.

I hurry down the hall. "Papa!"

If he's not dead, I may have to kill him.

I make it just past the library when a body yanks me inside the room, covering my mouth.

I jab the intruder with my elbow and stomp on his foot. He doesn't loosen his grip.

"You can come with me willingly or I can carry you out of here, kicking and screaming," Dante whispers into my ear.

I spin around and stare up into his dark gaze. I should hate him.

He lied to me.

Overpowered me.

He forced me to take that stupid little pill that saved my life. But I don't. All I feel is relief.

"Why?" It's all I can ask. The only word that finds its way onto my lips.

Dante is quiet for the briefest of seconds. "You're carrying my child. Do you really think I'm going to let you go on a date with that loser?"

"How did you know?" I pull him with me out of sight in case any of the guard's approach. "We have to get you out of here."

He laughs under his breath. "Only if you're coming with me."

I should be angry. Push him away. Tell him to leave. He invaded my house.

Except this isn't my house. At least not anymore.

I have no reason to believe that Romano lied to me, which means the monster I've been living with isn't Dante but my papa.

But I need to hear it from Dante. "Is it true?" I ask, staring up at him.

He shakes his head. He has no idea what I just uncovered.

"You told me Papa poisoned me. Did he also have me abducted? Is he the one trafficking women, girls, children?" My heart might burst out of my chest.

I thought Dante was the monster and maybe he is, but he's never been that way toward me.

I'm queasy, and Dante scoops me up into his arms before I can collapse. It's too much to bear.

"I'm taking you home with me."

He's not asking for my permission. There are gunshots inside and out. Is it safe to leave? Probably not, but his men are the invaders, and I am willing to go with him. Even held captive by Dante, he's more humane than my old man.

"Did you kill my papa?" I must know the truth.

"I gave the final order, but it wasn't my bullet."

39

DANTE

I expect anger, resentment, hatred, but that isn't what I find when I rescue Nikki.

Her arms are slung around my neck as I carry her out the front door, past the bloodshed and the bodies strewn all over the foyer.

It's not pretty. She doesn't even flinch.

I walk her back to my truck, outside the metal gates hidden from the surveillance cameras, and buckle her into the front seat.

Moreno can sit in the back. I'm being generous, offering him a lift back to the compound. He could drive back with Sawyer or one of the other men.

Several brought vehicles with artillery and soldiers prepared for war.

Moreno gives me a glance and a silent nod that all is good with my men.

The ride back is silent.

Every so often, I glance at Nikki. She's staring out the side window, quiet. I've never known her to be as silent as she is today.

Is she angry that we killed her father?

She hasn't spoken a word about it after I confessed to giving the order to have him executed. Most of his men on site were gunned down. A few fled, from what I heard over my earpiece, and my soldiers continue to hunt them down.

Will the DeLuca family finally be done once and for all in Breckenridge?

Nikki is the daughter of a mob boss.

Will she choose to take over her father's legacy? She doesn't seem the type capable of murder, and she isn't going to continue trafficking women.

What does that leave? Guns and drugs?

———

Moreno unlocks the front door, and I carry her into the foyer. She doesn't have shoes on, and the stone driveway and cement steps are hot even under the evening sun.

"I'll go up to my room," Nikki says the moment her feet touch the floor.

I grimace, not sure why she wants to go up to bed so soon. The adrenaline is still pumping through me at lightning speed. "Why? Are you feeling okay?" I ask.

She's been through a lot. I wouldn't blame her for wanting to take a nap, even though it's getting late.

It has been a long and probably exhausting day for her.

Nikki pinches her lips together. "I thought you'd want me out of your hair. I guess I'm used to being sequestered to my room."

My tight restrictions on her whereabouts in the castle will change. I don't believe she'll run again.

I could be a fool, but she has nowhere to go. No one to turn to, and she's pregnant.

She will have a guard posted outside of her room but it's for her own safety. I can't be too sure that the few men left won't try to retaliate.

"Well, if you can handle some dinner, you should join me in the kitchen."

She raises an eyebrow. "How do you know I haven't already eaten?"

Anything she'd have eaten would have probably come up already, given the events of the night. "Did you?"

I don't tell her that I stormed past the kitchen with a soldier, scaring the chef. He knocked over a half dozen dishes onto the floor when he threw himself onto the ground to hide.

She smiles sheepishly. "No."

"What do you feel like eating?" I ask. I'm not much of a cook, but I have a great chef on the premises.

"Soup, crackers, water, the usual."

No way. We're not playing that game anymore. "You're eating a healthy dinner. If I must take you out to dinner to help win back your appetite, so be it."

A smile quirks at her lips. She seems much more relaxed, comfortable. "You'll let me leave this place?"

"You're not a prisoner, Nikki," I say, wanting her to know the truth and accept it. "I never intended to buy you and keep you locked up. But once I found out that you were pregnant, I was concerned that I'd never see my child and that you would be a target."

She nods slowly, listening to what I have to say.

"You honestly mean to tell me that I can go out to the store, buy pregnancy clothes, get a latte?"

"Yes, yes, and after the baby is born, you can have as much coffee and caffeine as you'd like." That doesn't mean that I'll let her go alone. A guard will keep watch over her and protect her.

Her nose scrunches up in that adorable way that makes my heart pitter patter.

"I miss coffee," she whines.

"Well, that's good news. It means you have an interest in food again." I brush a strand of hair behind her ear.

She leans into my touch.

"Now, about dinner. What do you want to eat?"

"I have a mad craving for sushi," Nikki says.

I'm pretty sure a pregnant woman isn't supposed to consume raw fish. "Any other cravings?" I hate telling her no, especially after all she's been through.

"Aside from you?"

It's like she can read my mind. I pull her hard against me, and our lips crash together.

I'm grateful to have her back and in my home. It makes my heart soar to hear that she wants to be here, with me.

My fingers roam against her hip, under her shirt, grazing her skin. She's tiny and feels incredibly fragile.

I want to devour her, but not until after we've eaten. She's pregnant, and our baby and her health need to take priority over my needs.

It's the first time in my life I've ever put someone else first.

"Dinner," I say again between kisses. "What do you want to eat?"

Her face scrunches up, and she whimpers when my lips linger on her neck.

"Nikki?"

A soft hum emits from the back of her throat.

"Anything if it involves you naked and feeding it to me." The grin that she adorns tugs at my insides, and her words make my cock harden.

"Woman, you will be the death of me."

EPILOGUE

NICOLE

I have a son. For a moment, there was concern with Ace Fever, the stress of the pregnancy, and delivering early.

But holding Luca in my arms, feeling the overwhelming sensation of joy, without a doubt, I knew he would be okay.

And he is. He's perfect. Growing up fast, already toddling around, getting into everything imaginable.

Luca has his father's eyes, and every time I hold our son, he reminds me so much of Dante. The resemblance grows even more uncanny with every passing day.

Dante has been amazing as both a husband and father. For a man who is entirely alpha—protective and dominant, there's a gentler side that I was surprised to discover.

"How's my boy?" Dante asks as he lifts Luca into his arms and spins him around.

Luca sucks on his pacifier, unwilling to part with it no matter how hard we try to bribe him with stuffed animals and treats. I swear he'll be taking that damn thing to preschool in the fall.

Luca squeals with delight when Dante tosses him into the air. "You're getting too big for this." Dante grins and catches him low to the ground intentionally, pretending he's much too heavy and big.

"You two are going to give me a heart attack," I say with a laugh. I'm only half-joking. I try not to be the overprotective helicopter parent, but our line of work is dangerous.

Luca and Dante are my world.

I never thought I'd see the day when I would be married to a don.

"Any word on the DeLucas and Vance?" I ask, trying to be casual about my question.

Papa died during the ambush when Dante rescued me, and most of his men had perished in the assault that day. But Vance had escaped with two men in the forest, Marco and Rafael.

"I put Sawyer on hunting them down. Vance was spotted in Chicago and Rafael in California."

"Any idea why they're so far apart?" I don't want to worry about the business, that's Dante's job, but when it involves my ex-family, I worry that my son is a target.

"The Russians gave me a heads up about Vance, but no, I don't know what he has planned," Dante says. "I've got the best men keeping tabs on their whereabouts, and if they so much as cross over the state line, I'll know about it."

Exhaling a heavy breath, I lean in and steal a kiss from Dante. "I trust you."

"I know. I love you and trust you too," he whispers against my lips. "Oh, did you hear Moreno is getting married and having a girl? Can you imagine if our kids got married—"

"No," I cut him off before he can suggest what I think he's about to say. "No more arranged marriages. Our son can grow up to marry whomever he loves."

———

Thank you for reading Secret Vow. Continue the adventure with Captive Vow for Moreno's story.

Hired as a nanny...

Her father tells me she's mute. Except I catch her humming a lullaby.

He's a liar. Or she has everyone deceived.

What possibly could a four-year-old be hiding?

I really should have done a background check on him. Imagine my surprise when I discover my grumpy boss works for the mafia.

I want to leave but he won't let me. I'm his captive, forced to follow his rules and do as he demands.

One-click CAPTIVE VOW now!

Ready for your next one-click read? Binge the Eagle Tactical Series starting with Expose: Jaxson or grab the boxset Eagle Tactical Collection.

And sign up for my newsletter to find out about new books, giveaways, and freebies: www. authorwillowfox.com/subscribe

I appreciate your help in spreading the word, including telling a friend. Reviews help readers find books! Please leave a review on your favorite book site.

GIVEAWAYS, FREE BOOKS, AND MORE GOODIES

I hope you enjoyed SECRET VOW and loved Dante and Nikki's story.

Sign up for my Willow Fox newsletter

If you enjoyed SECRET VOW, please take a moment to leave a review. Reviews helps other readers discover my books.

Not sure what to write? That's okay. It doesn't have to be long. You can share how you discovered my book; was it a recommendation by a friend or a book club? Let readers know who your favorite character is or what you'd like to see happen next.

Thank you for reading! I hope you'll consider joining my mailing list for free books, promotions, giveaways, and new release news.

ABOUT THE AUTHOR

Willow Fox has loved writing since she was in high school (many ages ago). Her small town romances are reflective of living in a small town in rural America.

Whether she's writing romance or sitting outside by the bonfire reading a good book, Willow loves the magic of the written word.

She dreams of being swept off her feet and hopes to do that to her readers!

Visit her website at:

https://authorwillowfox.com

ALSO BY WILLOW FOX

Eagle Tactical Series

Expose: Jaxson

Stealth: Mason

Conceal: Lincoln

Covert: Jayden

Truce: Declan

Mafia Marriages

Secret Vow

Captive Vow

Savage Vow

Unwilling Vow

Ruthless Vow

Bratva Brothers

Brutal Boss

Wicked Boss

Possessive Boss

Obsessive Boss

Dangerous Boss

Bossy Single Dad Series

Billionaire Grump

Mountain Grump

Looking for kinkier books? Try these spicy stories written under the name Allison West.

Boxsets

Academy of Littles

Western Daddies Collection

Obey Daddy Collection

The Alpha Collection

Western Daddies

Her Billionaire Daddy

Her Cowboy Daddy

Her Outlaw Daddy

Her Forbidden Daddy

Standalone Romances

The Victorian Shift

Jailed Little Jade

Prefer a sweeter romance with action and adventure?
Check out these titles under the name Ruth Silver.

Aberrant Series

Love Forbidden

Secrets Forbidden

Magic Forbidden

Escape Forbidden

Refuge Forbidden

Boxsets

Gem Apocalypse

Nightblood

Royal Reaper

Royal Deception

Standalones

Stolen Art

Made in United States
North Haven, CT
25 August 2023

40737280R00193